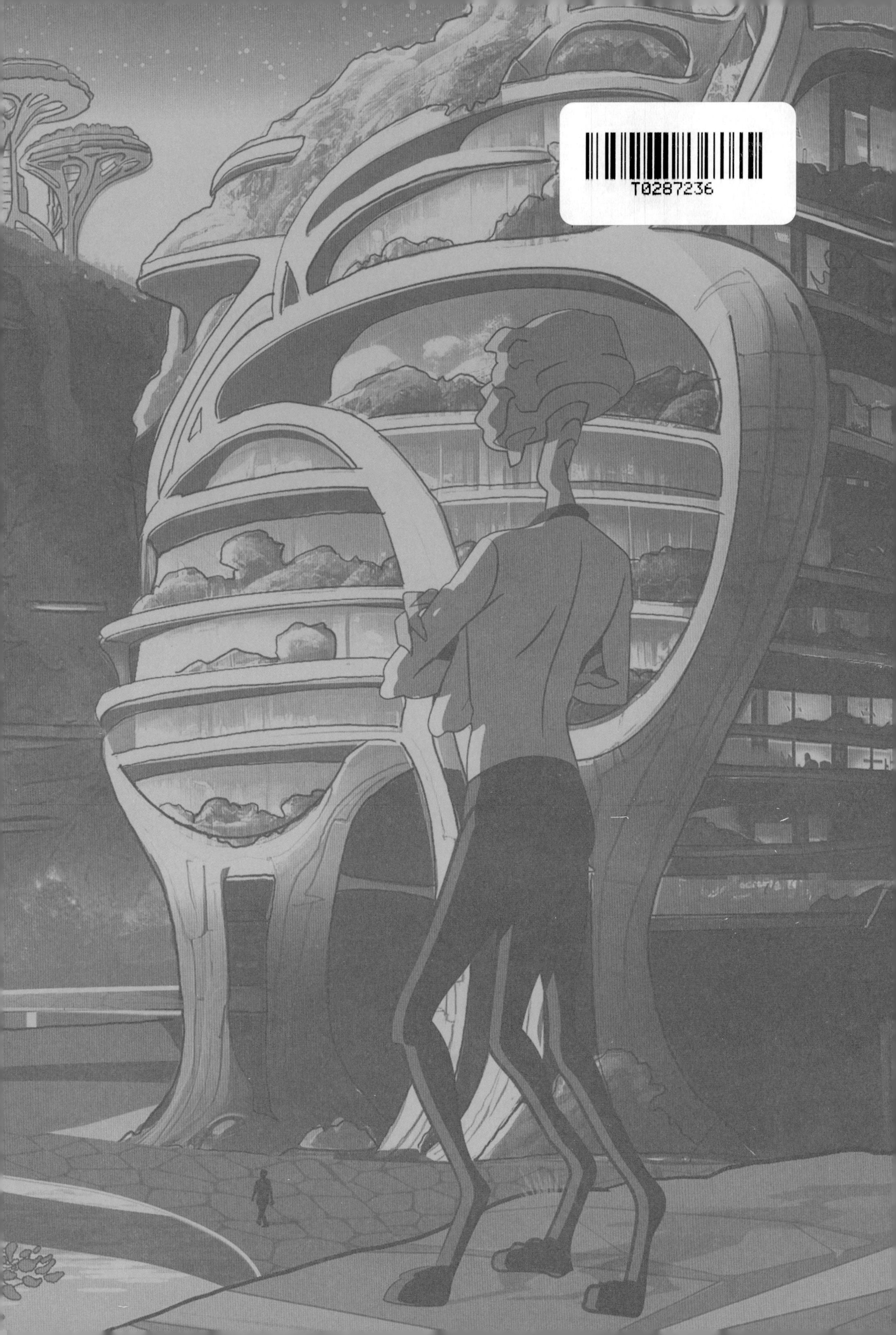

STAR TREK™
EXPLORER

THE OFFICIAL MAGAZINE

PRESENTS

"A YEAR TO THE DAY THAT I SAW MYSELF DIE" AND OTHER STORIES

STAR TREK EXPLORER

THE OFFICIAL MAGAZINE

PRESENTS

"A YEAR TO THE DAY THAT I SAW MYSELF DIE" AND OTHER STORIES

The short stories contained in the book feature characters and situations from across the *Star Trek* universe, including *Star Trek, Star Trek: The Animated Series, Star Trek: The Next Generation, Star Trek: Deep Space Nine, Star Trek: Voyager,* and *Star Trek: Picard.*

These self-contained stories include an adventure following the aftermath of *Star Trek: The Wrath of Khan,* co-written by Mr. Chekov himself, Walter Koenig, a trip into Vulcan history, and, for the first time, stories featuring Jack Crusher, Annika Hansen/Seven of Nine, and Captain Liam Shaw from *Star Trek: Picard.*

EDITORIAL
Editor: Jonathan Wilkins
Designer: Dan Bura

Group Editor: Jake Devine
Senior Creative Editor: David Manley-Leach
Editor: Phoebe Hedges
Assistant Editor: Louis Yamani
Editorial Assistant: Ibraheem Kazi

Art Director: Oz Browne
Designers: Donna Askem & David Colderley

Head Of Production: Kevin Wooff
Production Manager: Jackie Flook
Production Controllers: Caterina Falqui & Kelly Fenlon

Publicity Manager: Will O'mullane

Publicist: Caitlin Storer
Publicity & Sales Coordinator: Alexandra Iciek

Head Of Creative & Business Development: Duncan Baizley
Publishing Directors: Ricky Claydon & John Dziewiatkowski
Chief Operating Officer: Andrew Sumner
Publishers: Vivian Cheung & Nick Landau

DISTRIBUTION
U.S. Distribution: Penguin Random House
U.K. Distribution: MacMillan Distribution
Direct Sales Market: Diamond Comic Distributors

General Inquiries: customerservice@titanpublishingusa.com

Star Trek Explorer Presents "A Year to the Day That I Saw Myself Die" and Other Stories
ISBN: 9781787739642
Published by Titan Magazines
A division of Titan Publishing Group Ltd., 144 Southwark Street, London SE1 0UP,
TM ® & © 2024 CBS Studios Inc. © 2024 Paramount Pictures. STAR TREK and Related Marks are Trademarks of CBS Studios Inc. All Rights Reserved. Titan Authorised User. CBS, the CBS Eye logo and related marks are trademarks of CBS Broadcasting Inc. TM & © 2024 CBS Broadcasting Inc. All rights reserved. No part of this publication may be reproduced, stored in a retrieval system, or transmitted, in any form or by any means, without the prior written permission of the publisher.
A CIP catalogue record for this title is available from the British Library.
First Edition December 2024

10 9 8 7 6 5 4 3 2 1

Printed in China.

Paramount Global: Marian Cordry
Copyright Promotions Ltd.: Anna Hatjoullis
Paramount Home Entertainment: Kate Addy, Jiella Esmat, Liz Hadley, and John Robson

Simon & Schuster US: Ed Schlesinger

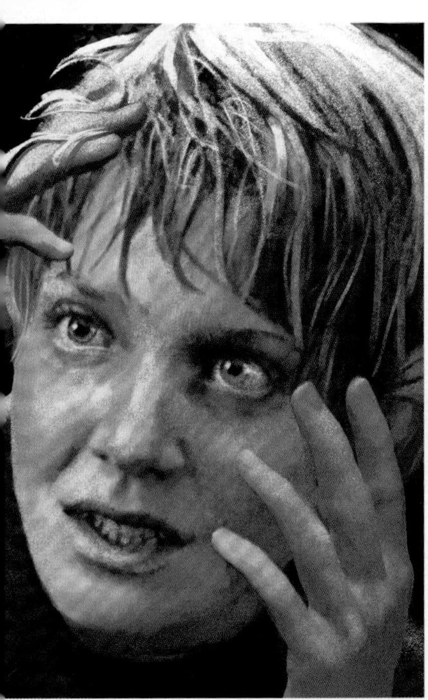
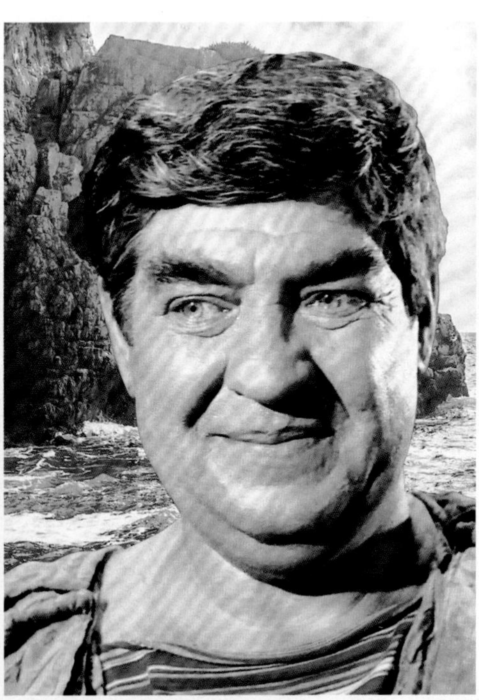
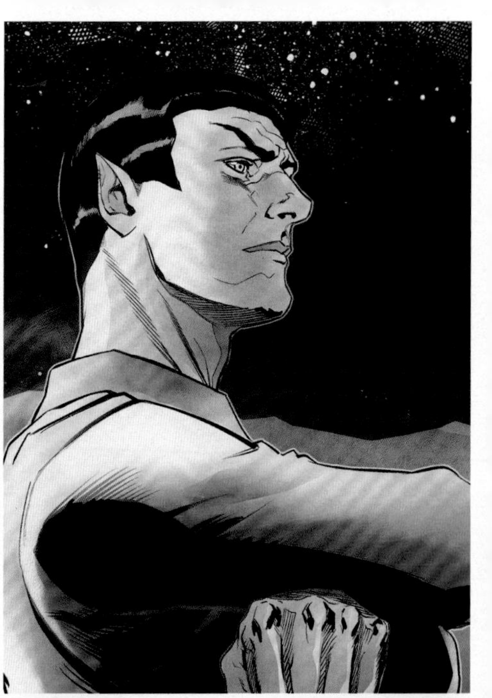
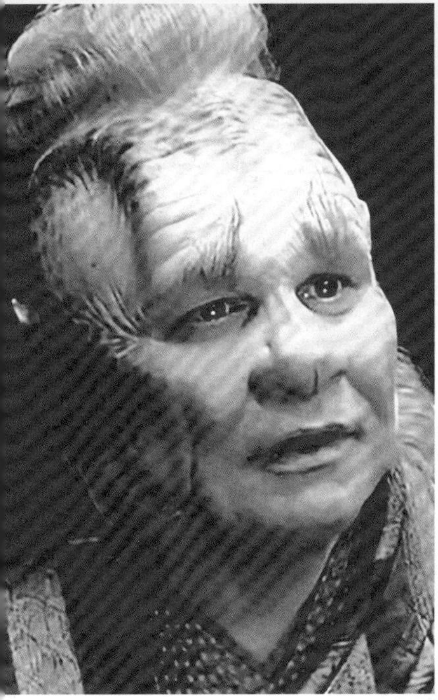
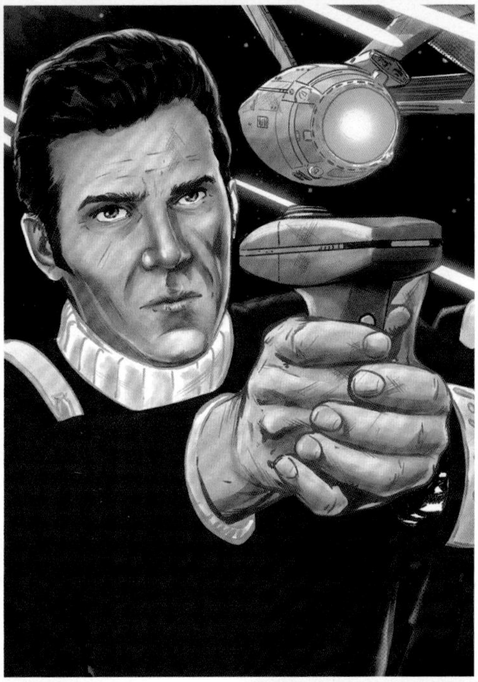
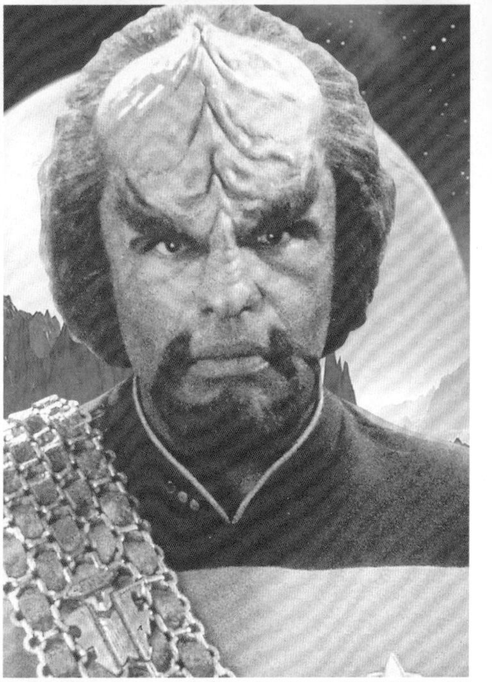
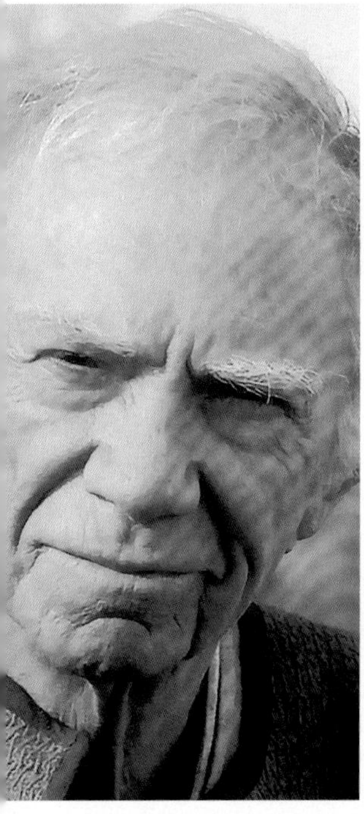
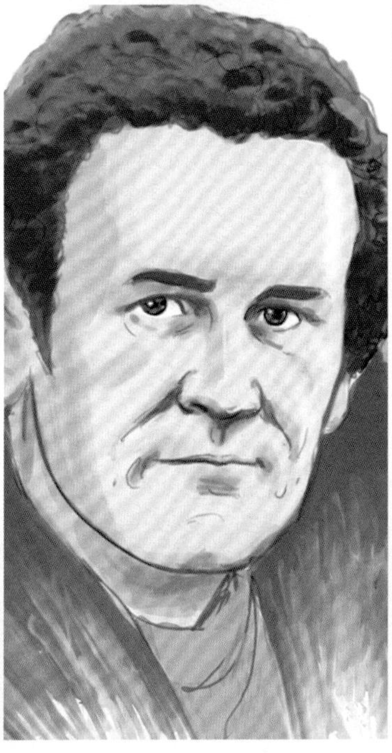
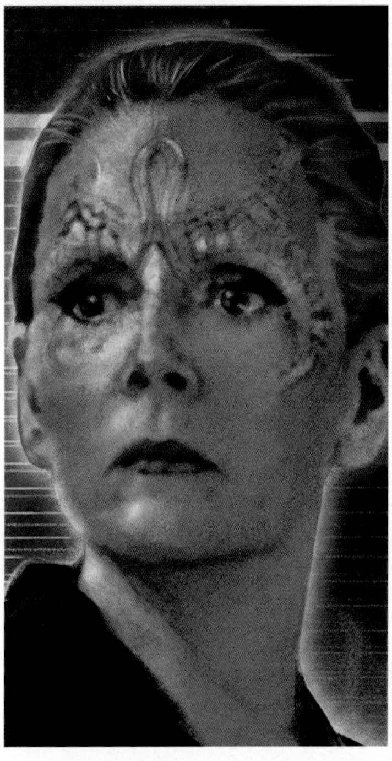
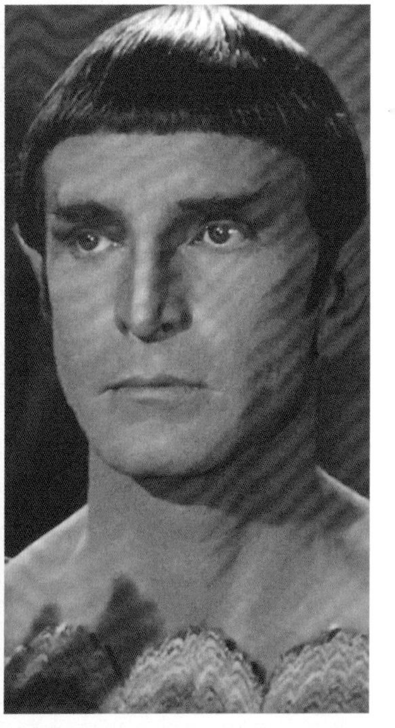

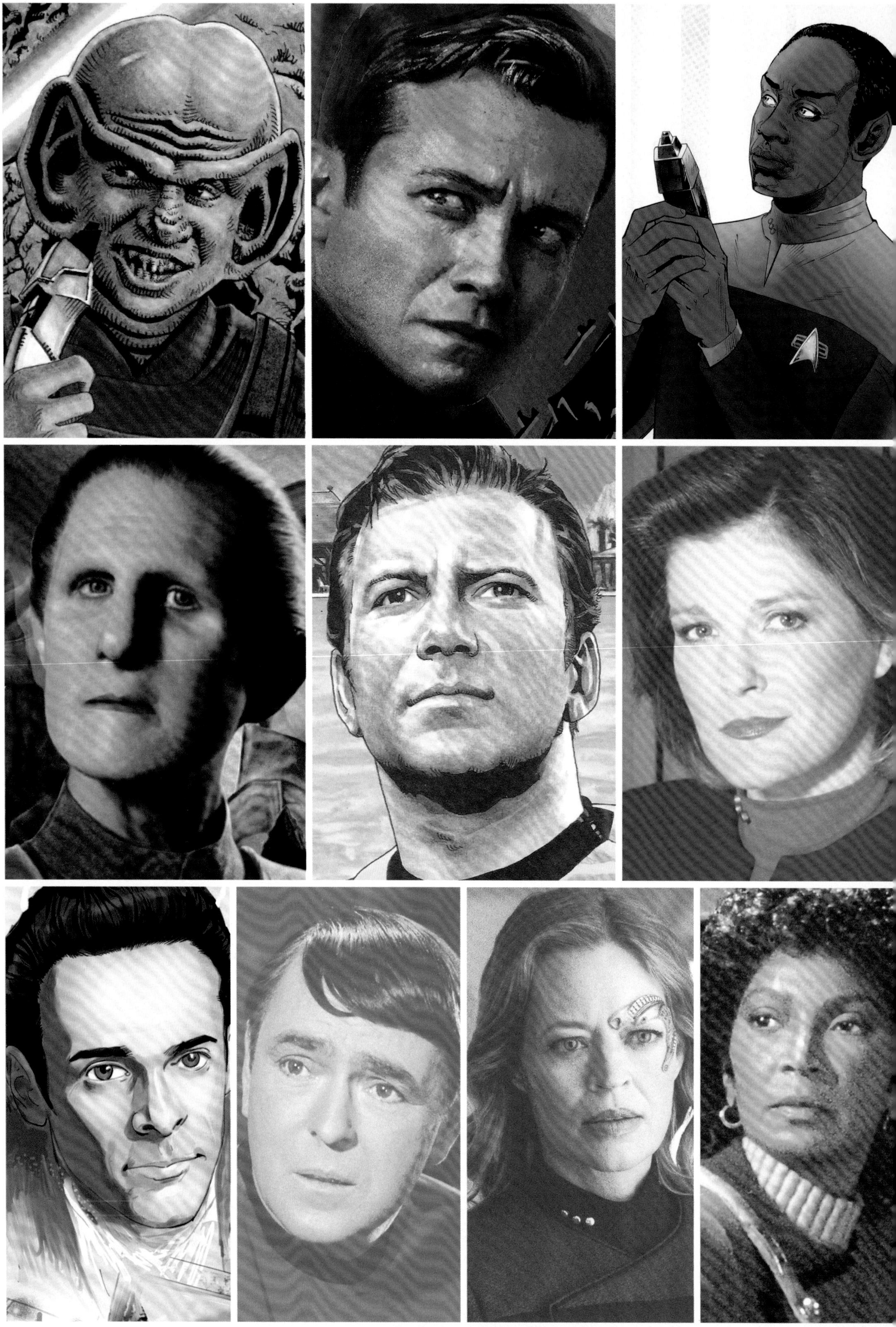

Contents

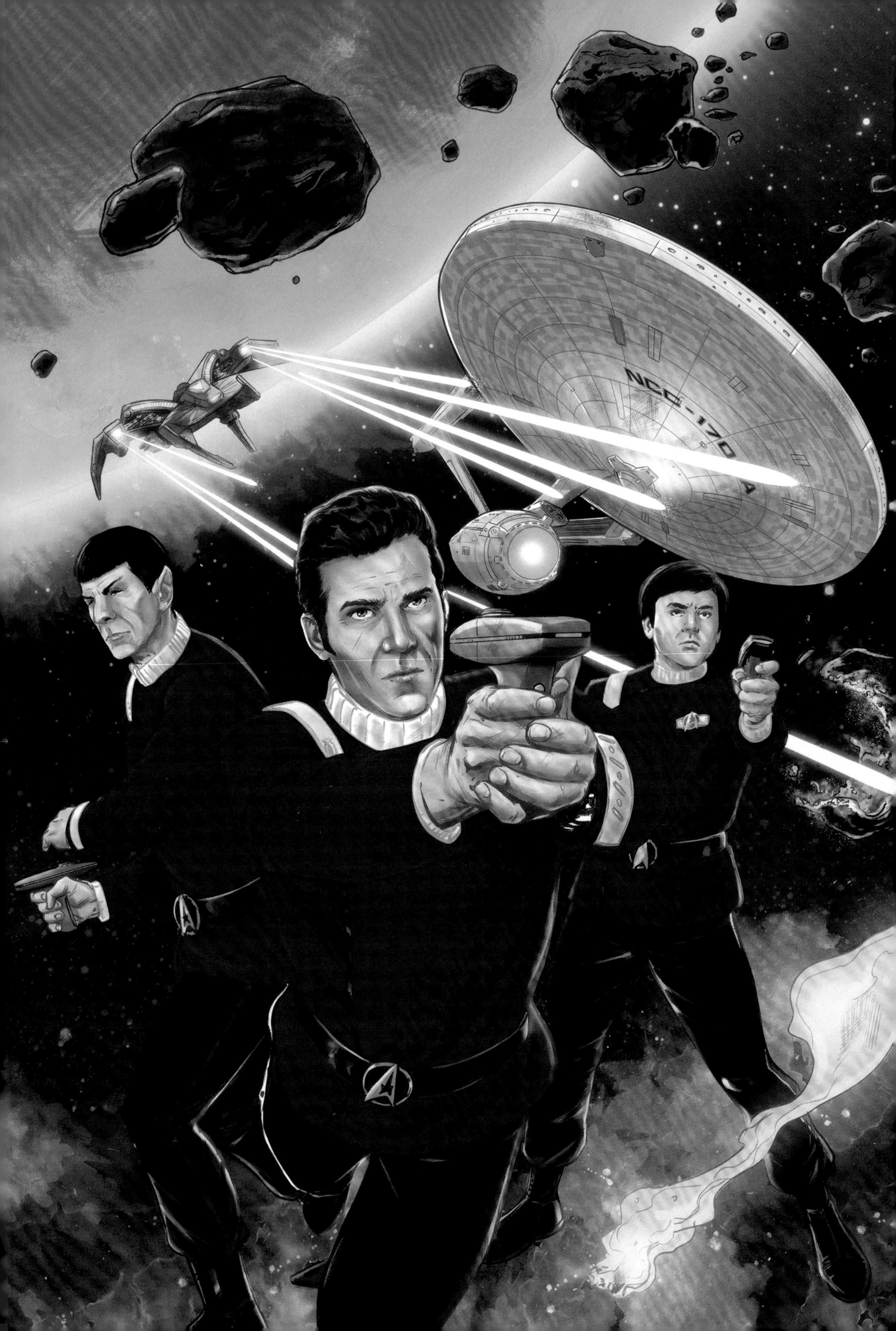
NCC-170

Chekov's Challenge

STORY: WALTER KOENIG AND CHRIS MCAULEY
ILLUSTRATION: NEIL EDWARDS AND JOHN PAUL-BOVE

STARDATE 8130

Commander Pavel Chekov stood by the viewport in his quarters aboard the *U.S.S. Enterprise*, his gaze was fixed upon the stars. The blurred points of light glinted across his eyes as the ship limped towards Earth Spacedock, still some light years distant. The *Enterprise* had been badly damaged in its most recent adventure, and Scotty had ensured that the senior staff knew that he was performing miracles in engineering, just to keep the ship at warp speed.

Chekov's thoughts turned inward, towards the weeks since the devastating events surrounding Khan Noonien Singh's return, and the sacrifice of Mr. Spock. Since joining the service, he'd always felt a passion for Starfleet's mission to explore the uncharted realms of the universe. As a younger man, the adventures he had shared with the crew of the *Enterprise* had always filled him with a giddy joy,unsure of what dangers he would face or wonders he would encounter as each duty shift began. He had taken those feelings with him during his short and ill-fated tenure with the *U.S.S. Reliant*.

Now, he closed his eyes and took a deep breath, trying to summon some of that excitement, but once again the memories of Spock's selfless sacrifice played in his mind like a haunting melody. The guilt that he felt about his part in Singh's plot was a perfect, bitter chaser. Although his mind had been controlled by a Ceti Eel, he couldn't help but feel that he could have done something different to prevent the events playing out as they did.

Suddenly, Chekov's reverie was broken, as a series of shocking explosions rocked the *Enterprise*. A red hue bathed his quarters and klaxons blared throughout the starship, as Chekov stumbled from his quarters and headed towards the bridge. Admiral Kirk spared the experienced tactical officer a glance as he rushed towards his position, Ensign Kelly gladly yielding the position.

"Glad to have you join us, Mr. Chekov." Even with the dire nature of the situation unfolding around them, Kirk managed to inject some warmth in his terse tone.

Chekov's fingers navigated around the tactical console. The sensor readings indicated that a lone Orion pirate ship – a Cruiser-class vessel – had emerged from a gaseous nebula ahead clearly lying in wait for them. The cosmic phenomenon had masked its approach, and enabled it to take the *Enterprise* by surprise. Chekov guessed that the pirate ship's sensors had detected the heavy damage the starship had sustained, and that its commander was an opportunist. Booty from a Federation ship would elevate a pirate captains' reputation – as well as their credit rating.

The *Enterprise* rocked again with the impact of the pirate ship's epsilon disruptor blasts. The ship's shields were holding, but Chekov knew that after their encounter with Khan, the ship's systems were only operating at sixty percent efficiency, and the barrage was already beginning to seriously compromise shield integrity. To make matters worse, weapons systems were still offline, its energy banks were being diverted to the warp core to maintain speed.

"Admiral, I can confirm from the pirate ship's signature that it's the notorious Orion marauder, the *Corsair's Revenge*." Uhura's voice rang out with its customary calm authority over the alert sirens continuing to sound on the bridge.

Kirk leaned forward, his eyes widening, and gave voice to the bridge crew's thoughts. Yet another dreaded enemy had returned from the past.

"Garroth!" The name conjured up past confrontations with the fearless pirate captain who now stalked his ship. The *Enterprise* had played a cat and mouse game with this commander decades ago, and Kirk remembered how dangerous a foe the Corsair had been.

Chekov thought back to that first encounter with Garroth, straight after the *Enterprise* had its near

devastating encounter with the Tholians. Echoing their position now, despite Scotty's best efforts then, the Tholian trap had left the starship's systems under strain, its crew vulnerable… and Garroth had taken advantage, with a sneak attack.

He shuddered, remembering how Garroth had jammed communication systems with his boasts of how he would destroy Starfleet's finest. That proved his undoing then, of course, his broadcast heard by the *U.S.S Yorktown*, who had sped to their aid and sent Garroth running, his ship badly damaged. But, he noted grimly, there was no such support for the *Enterprise* now, anywhere in the immediate area.

As Chekov desperately attempted to maneuver the *Enterprise* out of danger, the *Revenge* continued to unleash a series of devastating attacks. The tactical officer saw a spread of deadly photon torpedo's launch towards the *Enterprise*, and sweat began to form on his brow and top lip. The twin demons of doubt and fear, which he had so desperately tried to control, took hold of his mind. He wasn't sure, after all that had happened in the previous few months, that he was up to this task of helping defend the ship. Time

seemed to slow and Khan's face, with its cruel, mocking smile danced before his eyes. He felt sick to his stomach and a terrifying sensation of hopelessness washed over him.

It was then that he heard a familiar voice speak. It seemed to come from behind him. It was impossible but there was no mistaking the intonation or accent.

"SCOTTY, HOW LONG UNTIL WE CAN FIRE THE PHASERS? I WANT TO PUT SOME HEAT ON THAT ORION!"

"You can do this Mr. Chekov; I have full confidence in your abilities." The cool, logical voice of Spock cut through Khan's mocking laughter.

Chekov glanced over his shoulder, hoping to see his old Vulcan friend and mentor. Instead, he saw another familiar face. Admiral Kirk. The tactical officer noted Kirk's eyes were filled with a mixture of

determination and sorrow. He, of all the bridge crew had been the closest of all to Spock, and just like Chekov, had found his thoughts turning to his old friend in this moment of crisis. Kirk's eyes shifted to Chekov and for a second, they locked gazes. There was a silent acknowledgement between the two men and in that moment, Chekov found the strength to push his doubts aside.

The torpedoes barely missed the hull as Chekov expertly banked the ship sharply to the right. His focus sharpened and his mind cleared as his fingers danced across the controls. With each successful evasion, Chekov's confidence grew. He once again trusted in his training and the skills he had acquired over the long years of his Starfleet service.

"Scotty, how long until we can fire the phasers? I want to put some heat on that Orion!"

Kirk's question was answered with the Scottish burr of chief engineer.

"*Coming online now, Admiral. Fire away.*"

Kirk turned his head towards his tactical officer.

"You heard the man Chekov – use those phasers!"

Chekov responded with an emphatic "Yes Sir", as he eagerly touched

knew that detecting any weakness in their tactics could be the key to the *Enterprise* crew's survival.

The sensor readouts showed the energy fluctuations from the ongoing battle, the flicking of the shields as they were struck by deadly phaser weapons and the blips indicating photon torpedo exchanges. Then, something caught her attention, a subtle surge in the background energy patterns. It was as if there were disturbances in the fabric of space itself. She frowned; her intuition was telling her something was amiss.

"Admiral! I'm detecting unusual energy signatures. It's as if something is materializing *inside* our shields"

Her voice cut through the chaos of the bridge, and all eyes turned to her station. Kirk looked at Uhura with a serious expression.

"Elaborate, Commander."

"I can't be certain, but it's as though objects are phasing into existence within the ship shield's. It's highly irregular."

One possibility rang through Kirk's mind. It seemed impossible, but he couldn't take the chance that his instincts were wrong."

"Red alert! Intruders on board, all hands, prepare for boarders!"

Kirk's commanding voice echoed through the ship as the crew sprang into action. Security teams rushed to secure vital areas, arming themselves for the impending battle.

"Mr. Chekov, you've proven your tactical expertise time and again. I need you to take command of our security teams and repel those boarders!"

Chekov's eyes met Kirk's once again, with a quiet confidence.

"Aye, sir. I will defend the ship with everything we've got."

With a determined look, Chekov rose from his station and headed towards the turbolift unholstering his phaser and checking its energy banks along the way.

As Chekov departed, Kirk returned to the ongoing battle, knowing that his crew was in capable hands.

Chekov sprinted towards Engineering. It was logical that the marauders would coordinate their attacks there to effectively sabotage the ship. He observed crew members activating force field barriers at critical junctions, fortifying bulkhead doors and setting up impromptu barricades.

the phaser controls and unleashed a powerful wave of red energy. It struck the pirate ship, and the tactical officer restrained the urge to cheer.

"Direct hit, Admiral!" Chekov's exultant voice elicited a slight smile from Kirk. Something had happened during this battle. Some of the fire which he knew from the Chekov of old had returned. That was good, they would need it.

"It's a good start Mr. Chekov, but we aren't out of the woods yet."

As the battle raged on between the *Enterprise* and aboard the Orion pirate ship, its captain, older and wiser since his first encounter with the starship, long ago, realized that he needed to regain the upper hand quickly. Although the *Enterprise* was damaged, the reputation of Admiral James Kirk was not lost on Garroth. It was rumored that Kirk was one of the Federation's finest strategists and could always emerge victorious, regardless of the odds against him. The Orion ship's captain had no desire to be a part of Kirk's continued legacy.

Garroth barked orders to his crew in his native tongue, his first mate, a hulking Nausicaan named Grol was tasked with leading a boarding party. The Corsair would keep the *Enterprise* busy while

Grol and his team plundered the Federation ship from within...

"Prepare the boarding pods!" Garroth commanded in guttural tones and hisses. His eyes gleamed with reptilian avarice as he imagined the booty his crew would raid. "We'll exploit their damaged shields and slip through their defenses like a serpent in the grass… and I'll have revenge on Kirk, at last…"

The Corsair launched a fleet of small, agile cylinder-shaped transportation tubes which were directed towards the *Enterprise*. These pods were equipped with stealth technology which Garroth had cannibalized from the Klingons, making them nearly invisible to the sensors. Each pod carried a team of heavily armed pirates.

Meanwhile, Uhura's fingers flew across her control panel, as she monitored the Enterprise's sensors and communication frequencies. The tension on the bridge was palpable, as the intense battle raged on. Sweat broke out on the communication officer's brow as she focused on her task, her keen instincts and training honed to perfection. She, like Admiral Kirk, remembered the last encounter with Garroth. These pirates were formidable enemies, and Uhura

The ship's engineering teams worked in tandem with security to ensure that the intruders would encounter formidable resistance.

The pirates, clad in rugged, dark spacesuits cut through the ship's bulkheads with their weapons, and fanned out into the Engineering corridor. Their disrupter rifles were poised and ready, emitting a low, ominous hum. Each pirate's eyes scanned their surroundings, searching for signs of the *Enterprise* crew they had come to confront.

"Spread out, find their weak points, and remember to plant the charges near the Warp reactor core. We've a ship to plunder!" Grol's voice boomed towards Chekov and his security detail. They had hidden themselves against an alcove as the pirate crew had cut their way in.

Chekov scrutinized his team, checking their status. A few were seasoned officers who had served with the crew many years earlier. Most were raw cadets, on their first training mission when they gained brutal, bloody experience during their encounter with Khan. Each nodded towards their commander in turn, signaling that they were ready. Chekov slowly counted to three and then led his team out of the alcove and towards the pirates. With shouts of resolve the federation crew fired their phaser rifles at the enemy.

The pirates found themselves at a disadvantage and taken by surprise. They fought back, but the *Enterprise* crew were determined to defend their ship at any cost. The corridor echoed with the sizzling of phaser blasts and the menacing green blasts of disruptors.

Chekov's expertise also came into play as he directed his team to exploit the ship's layout for tactical advantages. Under his direction, they used cover effectively and employed suppression fire to keep the pirates pinned down.

"Hold your positions! We have the advantage. Keep the pressure on!" Chekov's voice carried above the noise of the battle and encouraged the security team to dig in and choose their targets carefully for maximum effect.

The Orion pirates, realizing that the tide of battle was turning against them, became increasingly desperate.

Some attempted to charge the crew in a reckless bid to break through the defense. Others sought refuge only to be flushed out by the determined *Enterprise* personnel.

Gradually, the crew's discipline, teamwork and superior numbers began to wear down the invaders. Phaser blasts found their marks and the pirates fell one by one, their disruptor rifles clattering to the floor.

Kirk pressed the communicator control on his command chair as the *Enterprise* rocked from the impact of the *Corsair's* photon torpedoes.

"Chekov, report. What's the status of our boarders?"

His question was met by the reassuring voice of his tactical officer.

"*Admiral, we've successfully repelled the pirates. There are a few stragglers, but our security teams are mopping them up now as we speak.*"

Kirk's shoulders visibly relaxed as he received Chekov's update. His voice carried a note of relief and pride as he responded.

"Well done, Mr. Chekov. Your leadership and the crew's bravery saved the day. Keep me updated on any further developments. Kirk out."

With that the communication channel closed, Kirk turned his attention back to the battle against the Orion pirate ship. His gaze narrowed on the viewscreen, where the pirate ship loomed. Outgunned by the *Enterprise*, Scotty, who'd somehow avoided the pirates in Engineering, was working miracles once more, he Orion vessel had taken severe damage, but the battle was far from over. Kirk's earlier relief now turned into steely resolve.

"Let's show these pirate scum that they've chosen the wrong ship to tangle with. Mr. Sulu, if I said Operation Solar Flare to you, would it mean anything?"

The helmsman thought for a moment before a smile creased his face.

"If I recall correctly, sir, this was a tactic from the early days… Captain Archer I believe. Required reading at the academy."

Kirk nodded and with a smile said, "At your discretion, helmsman."

Operation Solar Flare was a risky yet clever plan that would use the radiant power of the nearby star to the advantage of the *Enterprise*. The star was in its red giant phase, emitting intense bursts of solar radiation.

Kirk clicked a button on his chair to contact the Chief Engineer.

"Scotty, can you reconfigure the deflector shields to channel the radiation from the sun towards the Orion vessel?"

"*Aye, sir. But we can only handle that sort of energy for a short time. Perhaps only one or two blasts, Admiral – then we've had it.*"

"We've had it if we don't, Mr. Scott. Make the arrangements."

As the Corsair closed in on the *Enterprise*, Kirk ordered a series of evasive maneuvers. He needed to give Scotty enough time to reconfigure the deflectors, and also keep the Enterprise between the pirate ship and the red sun.

"All power to forward shields. Don't engage the Orion ship directly. Keep them focused on us." Kirk tried to hide the tension from his voice as he continued to direct his crew. They had one shot at this.

Sulu deftly navigated the *Enterprise* closer to the red giant, positioning it strategically to execute Kirk's plan.

"We are in position, Admiral."

Kirk pressed his communications button again. "Scotty – are you ready?"

The gentle Scottish burr confirmed that all the dishes had been reconfigured.

"Now, Mr. Scott –divert auxiliary power to the deflector dish and prepare to channel the solar radiation."

Kirk glanced at Sulu. "On my mark, Commander."

As the *Corsair's Revenge* closed in for what it believed to be its final assault on the *Enterprise*, Kirk saw his opportunity. He nodded to Sulu, who expertly aligned the ship with the star.

"*Now*, Sulu!"

At that moment, a massive solar flare erupted from the red giant, a searing burst of energy bathed the Orion pirate ship in a blinding wave of radiation. The pirate ship's systems overloaded, shields faltered, and its crew was left disoriented and vulnerable.

Kirk didn't hesitate. He ordered all available energy to be channeled into a devastating phaser volley directed at the now helpless pirate ship. Phaser beams converged, and with a blinding explosion, The *Corsair's Revenge* was engulfed in a cataclysmic fireball.

"That's the end of their piracy days." Kirk muttered, with some satisfaction.

As Sulu confirmed the destruction of the Orion ship, Chekov exited the turbolift and walked onto the bridge. Kirk greeted him with a nod and a heartfelt smile.

"There will be a commendation in my log for you, Mr. Chekov. Your actions saved the ship."

Later, as Pavel Chekov walked towards his quarters, he couldn't help but feel a sense of pride. He knew that Spock would have approved of his actions. Chekov had honored his fallen comrade through his courage and unwavering determination.

As he gazed out his viewport once more, Chekov still felt the keen ache of loss but it was now tempered with a newfound strength and resolve. The road ahead would be challenging but he felt a rekindled sense of hope. No longer burdened by doubt, Chekov had proven his worth in the heat of battle and felt a renewed purpose.

If his friends were beside him, he knew he could face whatever adventures the galaxy had in store. ★

"WELL DONE, MR. CHEKOV. YOUR LEADERSHIP AND THE CREW'S BRAVERY SAVED THE DAY."

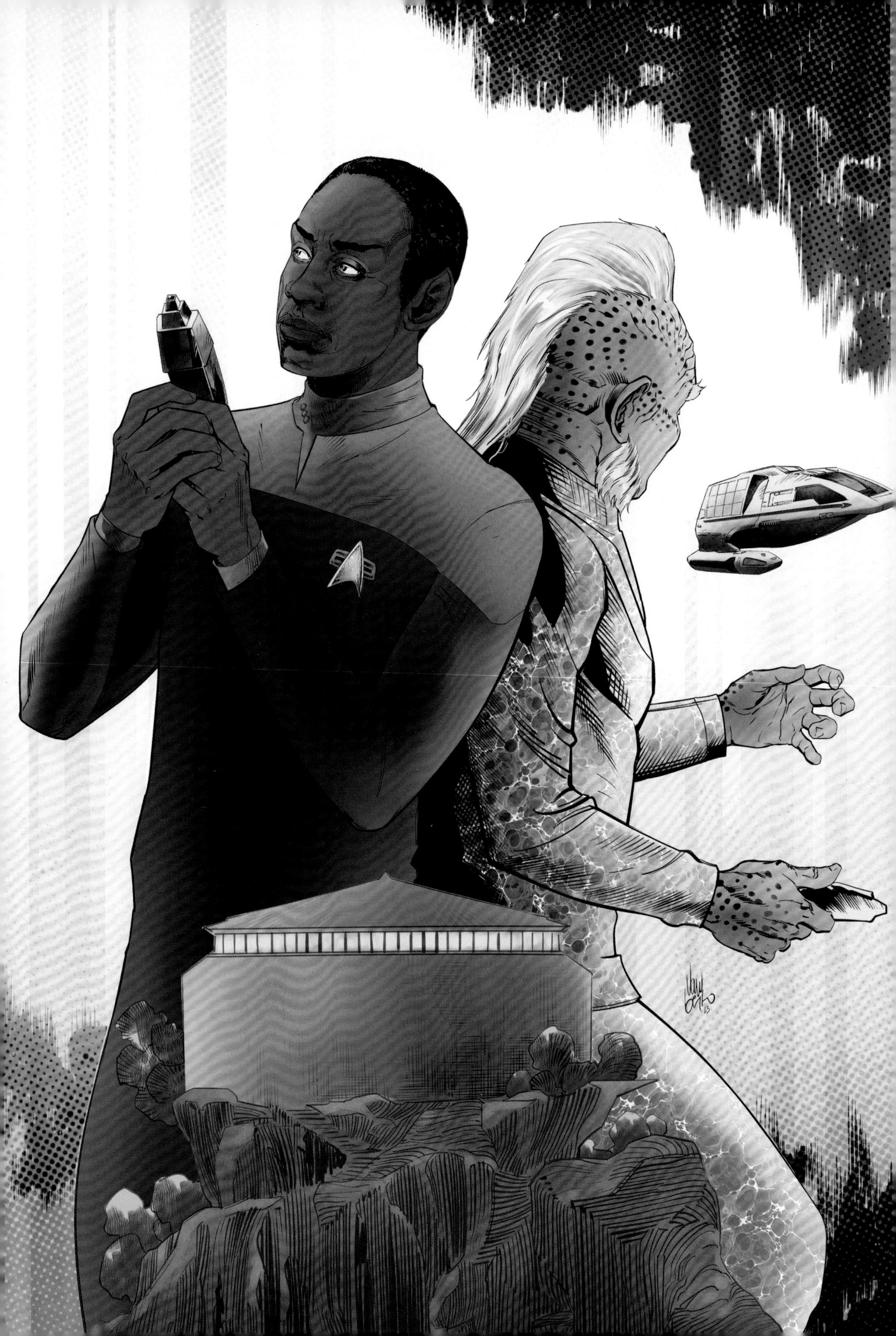

The Kellidian Kidnapping

STORY: KEITH R.A. DECANDIDO
ILLUSTRATION: WAMBERTO NICOMEDES

L ieutenant Commander Tuvok did not notice the explosive until 1.3 seconds before it detonated, which was an insufficient interval for him to act to prevent or avoid said detonation.

He lay under the pile of rubble, attempting to obtain sufficient leverage to shift the large piece of shattered mortar that was currently weighing down his thoracic region.

It had, he belatedly realized, been foolishly optimistic to believe that locating Captain Janeway would be as simple as tracking her combadge. He had been warned that the Kellidians were accomplished terrorists, and Tuvok was quite familiar with terrorist tactics. To that end, he should have anticipated that they'd leave the combadge behind as booby-trapped bait.

Once he had what he felt would be the proper grip, he extended his arms, removing the rubble from his person.

Tuvok sat up, gingerly. He closed his eyes and turned his mind inward, determining that he had several internal injuries. *Voyager* was in another star system, so he could not count on a Starfleet sickbay and the Emergency Medical Hologram to heal him.

Fortunately, he did not have to.

As he settled into the healing trance, he recalled how he found himself here...

"Captain's log, Stardate 53317.1. Commander Chakotay has taken *Voyager* to an asteroid field to mine for elements needed to repair the *Delta Flyer* after our encounter with the graviton ellipse. Meanwhile, I'm taking Lieutenant Commander Tuvok and Mr. Neelix in a shuttlecraft to Breva, a planet rich in exotic spices that Neelix would like to obtain for the galley."

As soon as Captain Kathryn Janeway finished her log entry, Neelix felt the need to put a word in from the passenger seat behind Tuvok and the captain. "The people I spoke to from the Brevan Trade Authority were most eager to do business with us, Captain. And ever since we came to this region of space, I've been hearing good things about Brevan spices. We should be able to make a good trade."

"I have faith in your diplomatic skills, Neelix," Janeway said with an encouraging smile.

For his part, Tuvok shared neither her faith nor her encouragement. They had only been in this region of space for a fortnight, having been thrust here unexpectedly by the subspace corridors used by the Turei and the Vaadwaur. However, he understood Neelix's psychology well enough to know how important it was to the Talaxian to feel useful on the ship.

Tuvok brought the shuttle to a landing in the clearing two kilometers outside Breva's capital city. Sensors detected three bipedal hominid lifeforms, as well as a medium-sized container, which matched what Neelix had said to expect.

Neelix stepped out of the shuttle first, Tuvok right behind him, scanning with his tricorder. Janeway exited behind Tuvok.

"Greetings," the Talaxian said, opening his arms wide and bending his knees in what almost looked like a curtsy, which Neelix had said was the customary Brevan salutation. "I am Neelix. You must be Chomforta."

The three Brevans all returned Neelix's gesture of greeting. Their epidermis were varying shades of golden, while their clothes were all incredibly bright colors and odd patterns, which reminded Tuvok unfavorably of the Hawai'ian shirts that Ensigns Paris and Kim inexplicably favored in the Paxau Resort holodeck program. All three wore shaded eyewear. The sun was shining brightly in the sky, so Tuvok understood the impulse. Each Brevan also had a device that resembled an old-fashioned communicator on their belt.

He was a bit concerned, as the container behind the Brevans was made of a substance that the tricorder's scans could not penetrate.

"I am indeed," Chomforta said in a pleasant tone. "Welcome to Breva."

Indicating the others, Neelix said, "This is Lieutenant Commander Tuvok, our chief of security, and, of course, our commanding officer, Captain Kathryn Janeway."

Tuvok merely inclined his head, but the captain performed the same gesture of greeting. "It's a pleasure to meet you."

"Trust us, the pleasure is ours." Chomforta nodded to one of his fellows, who removed his communicator.

Unexpectedly, a bright light burst from one of the containers. Tuvok was completely blinded and disoriented. He attempted to get his bearings while crying out, "Captain! Mr. Neelix!"

He heard the report of what sounded like a projectile weapon, and a scream that sounded very much like Neelix.

By the time his vision cleared, Tuvok immediately saw that the Brevans, the container, and Captain Janeway were all gone; Neelix lay on the ground, blood staining his jacket and pooling under his right shoulder; and Tuvok's tricorder was inoperable.

Tapping his combadge, Tuvok started to say, "Tuvok to Janeway," but the badge did not make any sounds upon contact with his fingers. Turning around, he saw that the shuttle's lights were dark.

Logic dictated that the Brevans used an electromagnetic pulse of some kind, hidden in the sensor-proof containers, and kidnapped the captain.

It would take the tricorder, combadge, and shuttle 2.7 minutes to reset themselves and reactivate. Tuvok took that time to minister to Neelix, using the shuttle's first-aid kit.

Once he had stanched the bleeding and given Neelix the appropriate medication, his tricorder was functioning once again. He quickly determined that there was no sign of the captain in scanning range.

Needing to dictate instructions to the shuttlecraft's onboard computer,

HE HEARD THE REPORT OF WHAT SOUNDED LIKE A PROJECTILE WEAPON, AND A SCREAM THAT SOUNDED VERY MUCH LIKE NEELIX.

Tuvok tapped his combadge again, this time receiving the telltale chirp. "Computer, contact local authorities for medical assistance to this location, as well as law-enforcement. And then send a distress call to *Voyager*."

"Acknowledged."

In contrast to the bright colors of Chomforta and his compatriots, Investigator Krimfrata of the Breva Lawgivers wore dark green clothing. He, too, had a communicator on his belt, along with a projectile weapon.

Tuvok and Neelix – the latter having been further treated by Brevan medics – sat across from Krimfrata, who said, "I'm sorry, but there is no such thing as the Brevan Trade Authority. However, we did receive a ransom demand from the Kellidians, saying that they have your Captain Janeway, and provided a list of demands – which I'm afraid we will not be fulfilling."

"Why not?" Neelix asked, sounding outraged.

"Because the Kellidians are terrorists. We do not negotiate with terrorists. The Kellidians have wreaked havoc all across the continent, and we will not provide them with *anything* save perhaps being bound by law and put on trial."

"But Captain Janeway – "

"Is not a Brevan citizen. You came to our world at the invitation of terrorists, I'm afraid you'll have to deal with the consequences yourself."

Neelix opened his mouth to argue further, but Tuvok spoke before he could do so. "Can you at least provide us with intelligence regarding these Kellidians?"

Krimfrata shrugged. "I can give you a map marked with locations where Kellidian activity has been detected. I'm afraid that's the extent of the cooperation we're willing to provide."

Tuvok and Neelix returned to the shuttlecraft. Neelix worked to contact the Kellidians to negotiate terms, while Tuvok searched for Janeway. The shuttle's sensors were unable to detect any human lifesigns, but eventually he found her combadge.

Sadly, it was booby-trapped.

Tuvok came out of his trance, satisfied that he had healed himself as well as possible. *Voyager* was still twenty hours away. But with every passing moment, the odds of Captain Janeway's continued survival decreased.

He returned to where they'd hidden the shuttlecraft to find Neelix at the fore console conversing with Chomforta, whose voice sounded over the shuttle's speakers. *"You will not be able to find us, Neelix. Your captain is somewhere you can't detect her. And you won't be able to trace this communiqué, either. If you don't provide the particle-beam weapons we requested by sunset, your captain dies."*

The transmission ended. Neelix turned to see Tuvok, eyes widening at the sight of the rips, tears, and green bloodstains on his uniform. "Mr. Vulcan! What happened to you?"

"The combadge was a decoy, left by the Kellidians to lure us to an explosive device."

"So my stalling them was useless." Neelix's shoulders slumped. "I've been a complete disaster on this mission."

"On the contrary," Tuvok said, "your stalling proved most useful."

"How's that?"

"Chomforta said that Captain Janeway was somewhere we cannot detect her. Logic dictates that she is being held in a structure made from the same material as the container the Kellidians hid their electromagnetic pulse flare in."

Tuvok sat next to Neelix and began the startup sequence for the shuttle to take off.

"I don't understand, how does that help?"

"I SAY AGAIN, THERE'S *NOTHING* TO NEGOTIATE."

"According to the information I've been able to glean from Brevan's public information system, the container is made of an extremely rare alloy known as crefarri." The shuttle started to rise up off the ground. "I will scan for sensor blind spots, and cross-reference it with the map Investigator Krimfrata provided."

Nodding in understanding, Neelix said, "And any blind spots that correspond to a place where there's Kellidian activity might be where Captain Janeway is!"

"Precisely."

"That's brilliant, Mr. Vulcan!"

Tuvok let out a sigh. Most non-Vulcans were inexplicably astonished at the application of simple logic, but Tuvok had always found Neelix's brand of astonishment to be particularly irksome.

Within an hour, Tuvok had checked every location on Krimfrata's map, and found only two blind spots. One of those was too small to block an entire human body, but the other was a structure only 1.2 kilometers from where the captain was kidnapped.

Transporters no more functioned through crefarri than sensors did. Tuvok would need to effect a rescue using more direct means. He was able to determine that there was no form of outer surveillance in the structure, nor even any windows. Tuvok couldn't see in, but the Kellidians couldn't see out, either.

"Computer," he said after a few moments' thought, "reprogram the aft sensor array to the following specifications…"

Kathryn Janeway had to admit to being impressed with the Kellidians. Their kidnapping operation had been very efficient, they knew enough to remove her combadge, and they had bound her with thick metal globes that engulfed her hands and were both attached to the wall. There was no way she'd be able to escape on her own.

She just had to hope that Tuvok and Neelix were up to a rescue. *Voyager* was a day away at maximum warp, so even if Tuvok had called for help – and, since that was standard procedure, Tuvok assuredly did so – it would arrive too late. Sunset was in about two hours.

A familiar voice sounded from outside. "Hello? Anyone home?"

"Who is that?" one of the Kellidians asked.

Their leader, Chomforta, said, "It sounds like Neelix. How did he find us?"

Janeway smiled. "I told you my people were good."

Chomforta ignored her and went toward the small door that was the only way in or out of this featureless building.

"What do you want?"

"To negotiate, obviously."

"There's nothing to negotiate. Give us weapons or your captain dies."

"Can you open the door, please? I think the negotiations will go more smoothly face to face."

"I say again, there's *nothing* to negotiate."

A pause, then: "You haven't given us any proof that the captain's alive. If you could just open the door and let me see her, we can move forward with getting you those weapons."

Turning to Janeway, Chomforta said, "Say something, Captain."

Janeway kept her mouth shut. She was hardly about to help them out, and besides, it was obvious that Neelix had good reason for wanting the door to be opened.

"You could've recorded her voice," Neelix said. "I need to *see* her."

With a snarl, Chomforta said, "Very well." He moved to open the door.

Janeway watched as he did so, and saw a most beautiful sight: Tuvok holding a phaser.

As soon as he was in view, Tuvok laid down phaser fire in a very specific pattern, shooting each of the seven Kellidians in the building – including the one standing guard on Janeway and the one in the far corner almost out of sight.

All seven of them fell to the floor, stunned.

"Nice shooting," Janeway said. "The one guarding me has a control key that'll free my hands." As Tuvok moved to retrieve that device, Janeway asked, "How'd you know where to shoot? I thought this building was made of sensor-proof material."

"It is," Tuvok said. "However, it is not proofed against temperature imaging."

Janeway frowned. "I've never heard of that."

"It was a form of surveillance used on Vulcan in the time before Surak. It detects objects on the basis of how much heat they give off. While crefarri is proof against sophisticated scanning techniques, it proved unable to stop this more primitive method. I was therefore able to determine where every single person was in the structure, so as soon as Mr. Neelix convinced the Kellidians to open the door, I was able to engage a specific firing pattern, that would stun all of your jailers."

Rubbing her wrists now that they were free of the metallic globes, Janeway said, "Very impressive, Tuvok."

"Hardly," Tuvok said with his usual modesty. "I was merely atoning for my previous dereliction of duty in allowing you to be kidnapped in the first place."

"I have to admit, I was surprised to see you two alone. I was hoping you'd be here with a contingent of Brevan security forces."

Neelix winced. "Unfortunately, Captain, they refuse to negotiate with terrorists, and they also were unconcerned with the welfare of aliens who were invited to their world *by* terrorists."

"I see." She sighed. "Neelix, how badly do you want those spices?"

"Not enough to want to spend another second on this planet, Captain."

"Good. Let's get the hell out of here." As she moved toward the exit. "And Tuvok, maybe you can tell me what happened to your uniform…" ✦

Lost and Founder

STORY: DAVID MACK
ILLUSTRATION: PETE WALLBANK

4491 A.D.

The dispersed essence of what once had been the Changeling known as Odo rode the leading edge of a derecho as it swept across a dry and lifeless plain. Eons had elapsed since Odo mastered this, the most difficult of his people's abilities. Altering his mass to take any individual form he desired had marked only the beginning of wisdom.

In the second millennium of his life, he had learned to scatter himself without losing control of his constituent atoms. The development of that skill had been a boon greater than anything he could previously have imagined. Instead of casting himself as a single stone, he could become a million motes of dust borne aloft on the arms of the wind, or diffuse his gelatinous form to reach every nook and depth of an ocean without a name.

Why become a fish when one can be the sea?

The key had resided in learning to sense and control the delicate bioelectrical field that united every particle of his being, and which also made possible the unions of two or more of his kind within or without the Great Link. His companions in the Great Link had called that tenuous field "the subtle body."

What I wouldn't give to hear the voice of my people once more.

It had been roughly two thousand years since the sundering of the Great Link, followed by the galactic diaspora of the Changelings. Once known as the Founders, they had ruled several dozen sectors of the Gamma Quadrant as gods. Then they had abandoned their empire, along with its billions of beings whose lives they had engineered to require their absolute control, broke all bonds of union with one another, and scattered themselves to the stars.

Odo had not seen another Changeling since that day, so very long ago.

Thus had begun his wanderings.

At first, he had searched for those who had left him, but they had left no traces, no clues, no sign they ever wanted to be found. He had roamed from one wandering star to the next, never finding what he sought. Instead, he had propelled himself only that much farther from his home.

Home. What did that word even mean anymore? Was home the Alpha Quadrant? The Gamma Quadrant? The Great Link? Bajor? No answer satisfied Odo's yearning.

Deep in the shadows of his mind lurked memories of the space station Deep Space 9, previously known by its Cardassian name, Terok Nor. Odo harbored a nostalgic attachment to that place, but his recollections now were all bittersweet. The last remnants of that station had been scrapped, melted down, and sold off centuries earlier. Nothing was left of it now but tall tales told by those who had never seen it or the Bajoran wormhole with their own eyes.

Shaping himself into a trickle of water, he merged with a small stream and let it carry him, pulled by gravity along the path of least resistance to the nadir of a valley, where it emptied into a brackish pond. Sensing the change in the water, Odo separated himself from it and went ashore in his golden gelatinous form. He coalesced at the pond's edge. Looking down, his gaze was met by that of his soft-featured reflection on the water's black surface.

Around him and the dark pool stretched desolate hills and barren plains touched by nothing but this world's churn of ceaseless wind. Sand funnels spun up without warning, whirled like dervishes, then tore themselves into quickly dissipated clouds of dust.

That was life reduced to its essence, in Odo's experience. Forms emerged out of chaos, sparking great flurries of action and struggle … only to exhaust themselves and collapse back into the dust and darkness from which they sprang. The same story, over and over again. Such was the arc of history, which bent not toward justice but toward entropy.

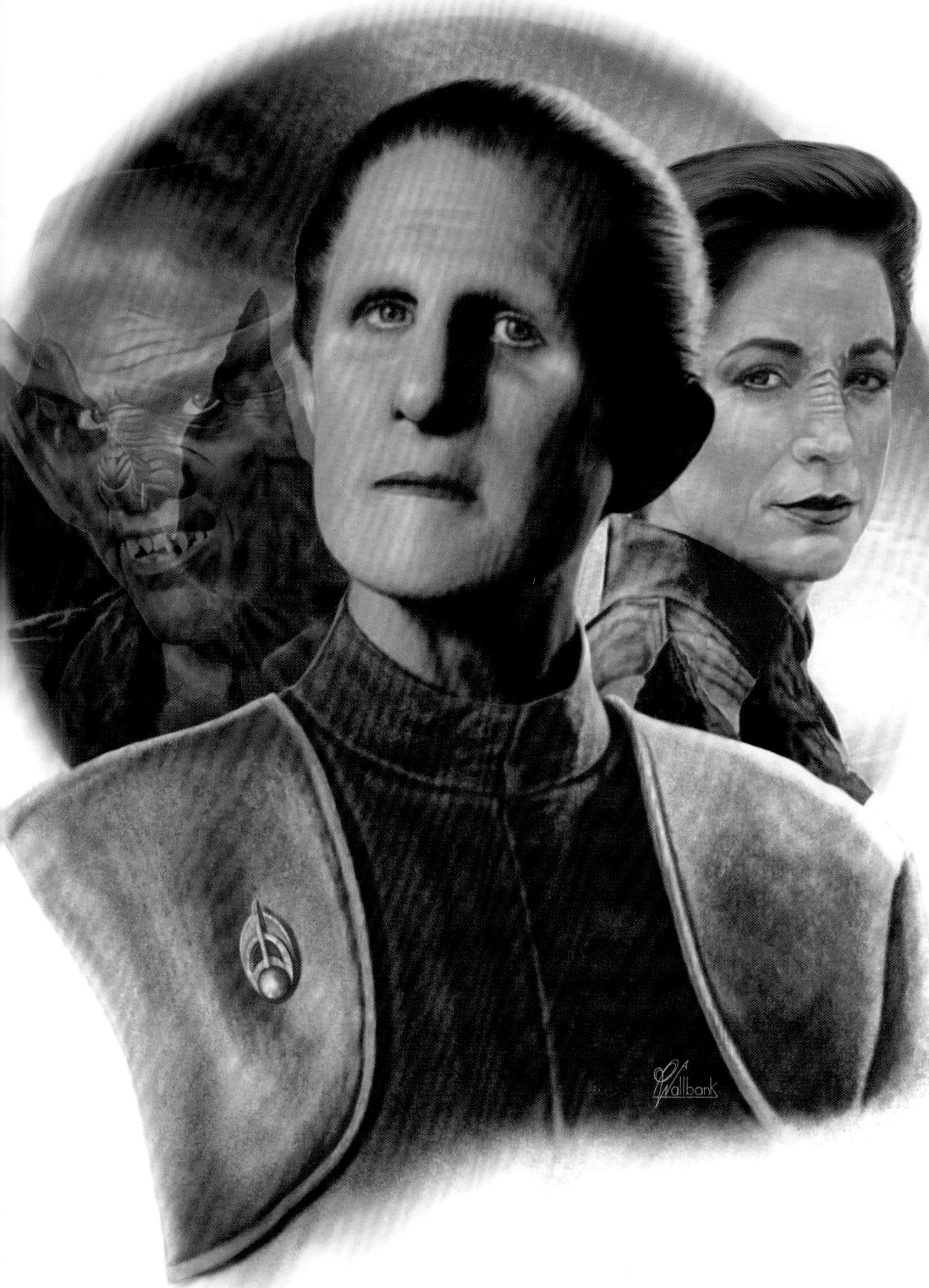
Wallbank

Throughout the universe, changes were never permanent—but change itself, as an inescapable force, was.

The pale, feeble disc of this world's white dwarf sun slipped beneath the horizon. Overhead, the blanched sky dimmed until the starry sprawl of the cosmos revealed its cold majesty. Odo turned his longing gaze upward, toward pinpricks of light that had travelled   hundreds, thousands, or even millions of years to reach him here, now, in this lonely place.

If only I had someone … anyone … to share this with me.

In the back of Odo's mind, behind the curtain of his thoughts, the murky ghost of a memory took shape. Then it appeared before him, standing with him at the water's edge: a humanoid form shining like molten gold as it grew and solidified.

He felt the invisible, gossamer-like thread of quantum consciousness that linked the being to his own essence; he was observing a projection made manifest by his unconscious mind, a phenomenon he had encountered several times in centuries past. The first time it had happened, its appearance had alarmed him. Successive encounters had led him to resent it as a cruel form of self-deception and torture. Only after

decades of introspection had he come to accept it for what it really was: a coping mechanism for nearly a millennium of loneliness.

Though Odo had met many thousands of persons in his two millennia of travels across the galaxy, he knew who his mind would conjure to keep him company. To paraphrase an old Earth aphorism shared with him long ago, he loved best those whom he had loved first.

"Hello, Captain."

Benjamin Sisko – or, at least, Odo's conjured doppelgänger of him – wiped his hand over the top of his shaved-smooth head. He was dressed in the Starfleet uniform in which Odo had last seen him, mostly black with a band of command red across his shoulders and the top of his chest. The human man's rich, umber-brown skin made his bright, wide smile pop in contrast as he acknowledged Odo's presence. "Odo! How good to see you." His voice was as rich and resonant as Odo had remembered, and the glimmer of optimism in

Sisko's eyes was undimmed by time. He took in their surroundings with friendly curiosity. "Where are we?"

"Somewhere without a name. At least, none that I know of."

Sisko creased his brow in a display of good-natured concern. "You look upset, Constable. Is there something I can do to help?"

"Can you tell me why I should go on living?"

His question seemed to amuse Sisko. "Why would I know that?"

"You're the Emissary of the Prophets."

"Not a role I chose. I never claimed to be anything but a man."

Desperation welled up inside Odo and put a vibrato in his gravelly voice. "But they showed you things. Told you things."

Sisko shrugged. "Riddles, mostly."

"*Hrmph.* I thought if anyone would know the secrets of the universe, it would be you."

"Sorry. The Prophets tended to leave me with more questions than they answered."

"WHAT WILL OUR COURAGE MATTER WHEN ALL THAT'S LEFT OF US IS DUST?"

Odo squatted beside the still water and considered his dim, starlit reflection. "Why does nothing ever last?"

"Because nothing can. Not forever." Sisko turned his eyes toward the stars. "Not space. Not even time. The seeds of our endings were planted at the moment of creation."

"*Now* you sound like the Prophets."

Sisko sounded amused. "I know you don't mean that as a compliment, but I'll take it as one all the same."

A gentle breeze swept over Odo, pelting him with dust and scattering his reflection on the pond's surface. "How am I supposed to live when I know everything is doomed to die?"

The masculine voice that answered him was deeper than Sisko's: "With honor."

Odo turned and looked back to see that the visitor from his

unconscious mind had reshaped itself into the likeness of Worf, as he had looked when he was in his prime aboard Deep Space 9. He wore a metallic baldric diagonally across his barrel chest and held his bearded chin high.

"*Honor*. Is that all you have for me after two thousand years? That same old refrain?"

"Call it what you want."

"I call it *delusion*. A lie used to mask a terrifying truth."

"Which is?"

"Nothing we do matters, Worf. One good man can't fight a corrupt regime. Or stop the strike of a planet-killing asteroid."

"True. Death comes for us all. None are spared."

"But you'd have me believe that it makes a difference *how* we die?"

"How we die matters as much as how we live. Perhaps more. The end is important in all things. To die bravely, we must first learn to *live* with courage."

Odo scooped up a handful of sand. With a slow turn of his wrist, he let it slide from his palm. "What will our courage matter when all that's left of us is dust?"

A richly mischievous feminine voice replied, "Who says dust is all there is?" An avatar of Jadzia Dax had supplanted Worf as his companion. The tall Trill woman's long brown hair billowed in the gentle wind. "Maybe death is part of a transformation beyond understanding."

Her suggestion surprised Odo. "Are you suggesting death is *not* the end?"

She shrugged. "There's a great deal we don't yet know about consciousness. Even with FTL sensors we've found it hard to pinpoint the origin of free will."

Odo's mood turned skeptical. "Jadzia, there's a universe of difference between the limitations of neurological science and the leap of faith required to believe in life-after-death."

"Is there really?" Her face brightened as she continued. "What if parts of consciousness we don't understand are rooted in quantum mechanics? For instance, imagine that a copy of our minds – our souls, or our *pagh* if you believe in such a thing – exists in a parallel quantum reality, one without our bodies, where we exist as pure energy. And when we die, instead of all we are

being lost forever, that other part of us, the quantum-entangled particles of our disembodied soul, persists in this other reality, aware of both itself and of the dispersed nature of our finite physical shells. It's not that far-fetched an idea. We already know parallel quantum universes exist, more than we could ever count, and that they constantly branch off into new possibilities. What if, for some version of ourselves, death really *isn't* the end?"

Odo stifled a derisive chortle. "I expect more from a science officer than fairy tales."

"Perhaps," replied Cardassian spy-turned-exile Elim Garak, "you have no appetite for sweetened lies because you've dined for so long on bitter truth."

"As if *you* would know anything about *truth*."

Of all the ghosts his mind tended to summon, the only one he disliked was Garak. The not-so-simple tailor represented the part of Odo's imagination that doubted himself. That lied to himself. That made him question his own judgement and sanity.

"If you won't listen to him,

maybe you'll listen to me," said the spectre of Quark.

"Not likely."

"Well, you should. Because I'm the only one who'll tell you the way it really *is*. The point of living is to *keep on* living. To *not die*."

Odo scowled. "What kind of empty philosophy is that?"

"The only honest one. Living things fight to survive because living is better than *not* living. Drawing breath is better than rotting in the ground. Existing is better than oblivion."

"Says someone who's never known real pain. Never felt the cruel grip of chronic suffering, or the crushing grief of permanent loss."

"YOU TAKE A FEW BAD HITS, AND NOW YOU WANT TO GO BACK TO YOUR QUARTERS AND CRY IN YOUR BUCKET."

Quark folded his arms across the front of his gaudily bedazzled tunic. "And you have?"

Too many memories rushed back at once and caught Odo unaware.

"I've seen entire civilizations exterminate themselves. I bore witness to a gamma-ray burst that sterilized a lush green world of every trace of life. Saw a supermassive black hole devour star systems like a predator eating its weakling young. I've borne witness to death and destruction on scales beyond imagination."

He heard somber compassion in the voice of long-dead Starfleet medical officer Doctor Julian Bashir: "We've all had to confront death at one time or another. It's a part of life."

"Death is *larger* than life, Doctor. It always has been. That's why it always wins."

Bashir scrunched his brow, clearly dubious. "Not always."

"On a long-enough time scale? Always."

"That seems unnecessarily reductive."

"Doctor, do you know what the difference is between stories with happy endings and those with tragic ones?" He looked at Bashir. "Where the author chooses to stop the telling."

The good doctor dissolved into a flurry of golden motes that sank into the ground, even as Odo felt another memory-golem solidify behind him. He pivoted to see the sweetly smiling face of young Ezri Dax, as she had looked during her first days aboard the station. "You don't really believe that, do you? I mean, look at my story. The death of Jadzia was a tragedy, but it wasn't the end. Her ending was my new beginning."

"You say that like you expect to live forever. As if you and your symbiont aren't doomed to be parted one day." Odo looked up at the night salted with stars but found no joy in it. "I saw the Burn wipe out every active dilithium crystal in the blink of an eye. It turned vast, interstellar civilizations into silent seas dotted with ten thousand lonely islands, each one alone in the dark."

"But they didn't give up," insisted Jake Sisko, the innocent, optimistic son of the Emissary. His was the voice of hope that had never wavered. "They held on. And they found a solution. The Federation rebuilt itself. As long as there's still life, there's *hope*."

It was so simplistic. So unsuspecting. The naïveté made Odo despair.

"I've seen alternate realities unravel like poorly woven tapestries. Universes filled with beautiful possibilities erased by the whims of 'higher beings.' What I've rarely found, on any world, is justice. And I don't know that I've ever found hope."

A stone skipped across the black water, bouncing thrice before vanishing beneath the surface, which now shimmered with intersecting rings of disturbance. Turning toward the source of the thrown rock, Odo found the solid apparition of Miles O'Brien, his engineering uniform scuffed and stained, his sleeves rolled up past his elbows. "So, you're just gonna quit, then?"

"I don't follow, Chief."

"The universe didn't turn out to be puppy dogs and rainbows. Life wasn't all beer and candy. Now you're mopin' about, feelin' sorry for yourself. I get it."

"Moping?"

"You heard me. You take a few bad hits, and now you want to go back to your quarters and cry in your bucket. Does that about sum it up?" He flung another flat stone across the pond.

"I haven't needed that bucket in nearly seventeen centuries."

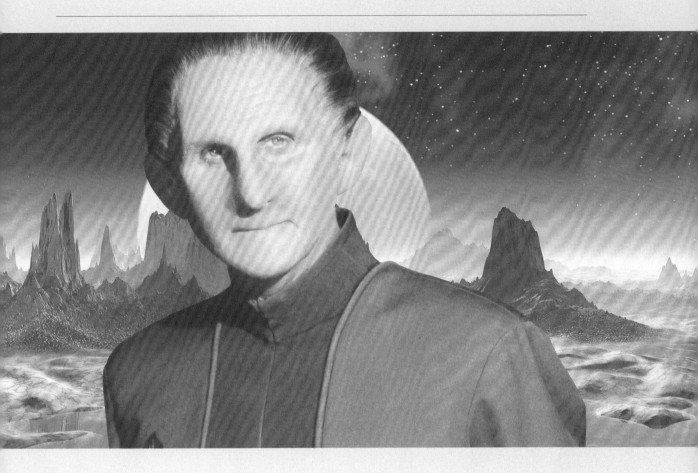

"Fine, go cry in your Great Link for all I care. But when you're done, get back to work."

"That's your sage advice?"

"We all have to serve something, Constable. A person. An idea. An institution. Something greater than ourselves. That's what gives us meaning."

Odo found no wisdom in O'Brien's counsel, only anguish. "Everyone I've ever known has grown old and died." He kneeled beside the dark water once more. "The only constant I've ever found is that life makes the same mistakes, over and over again. I've seen life betray itself so many times that I've forgotten why I ever cared about any of it. Or why I ever should again."

The answer came in the one voice that Odo missed most of all.

"You know why."

He turned away from his reflection to face her. "Nerys."

She was eons gone, but there she stood, her brown eyes clear and bright with purpose, her voice as steady as bedrock. The hint of a

breeze teased shocks of her short auburn hair into motion. Though in life she had eventually traded her military garb for the robes of a vedek, today she stood before Odo in the uniform she had worn during their last several years of shared service on Deep Space 9. Her smile was gracious and genuine. "Hello, Odo."

Though his Changeling form had no lachrymal glands, centuries of learned behavior caused Odo's eyes to glisten with ersatz tears, and his voice shook as he fought to rein in his emotions. "I've missed you so much, Nerys."

"I've missed you, too. But I need you to remember."

He nodded. "Our conversation."

She took his hand. "And your promise."

Too ashamed to look her in the eye, he stared at the ground between them. "I've tried. But time is cruel, and the cosmos is rigged against us. Against life itself. How am I supposed to hold on to hope in a universe so bereft of compassion? So devoid of meaning?"

Kira reached up with her free hand and pressed her palm against his cheek. He found the warmth of her touch comforting, even though he knew it was just a facsimile built from his own memories. Then she kissed him: softly, and tenderly, but also passionately enough to make him forget nearly two thousand years of sadness and bitterness, even if only for a moment.

"Remember the only thing that ever really matters. The one thing that gives meaning to our struggles against the darkness, as futile as they might be. *Remember*."

"I will," he promised her.

As he had thousands of times before. As he would countless times again.

He watched the only person he had ever loved dissolve into dust.

His face was still warm where she had touched him. Clinging to her memory, Odo sat down beside the dark, still water. Alone beneath a cold and unforgiving sun, he mustered the faintest ghost of a smile … as he remembered *love*. ★

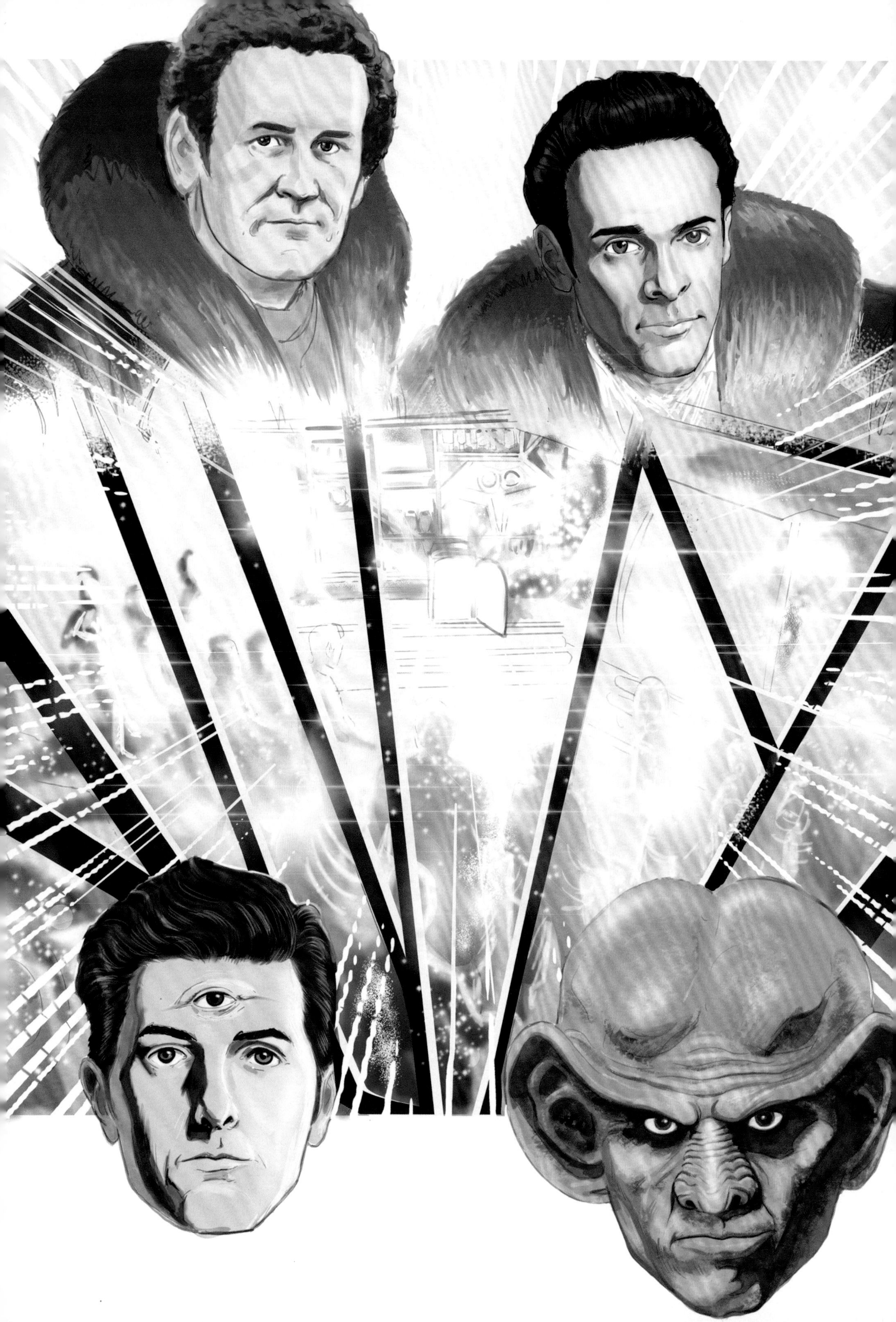

A Year To The Day I Saw Myself Die

STORY: MICHAEL COLLINS
ILLUSTRATION: MICHAEL COLLINS

ILES!"

*And it's his father, his **Da**, silhouetted in the doorway; and it's Miles – 13 now – in his childhood bedroom in Dublin,* knowing he's in it for missing cello practice because he got distracted fixing the gravlift on Declan Shalvey's flipboard. The dream is so intense –

BUT
"Miles!"
It's not his Da.
"Miles!"
It's himself.
And it's not Dublin, it's Deep Space 9.
And the Miles in the doorway is dying.

Chief Miles Edward O'Brien wakes with a start, he's sweating, alarmed- the dream still so close and so real he can smell the static from the time apparatus on his dying self.

He checks the station's chrono- and there it is. A shudder runs through him.

He thinks to himself : "A year. A year to the day I saw myself die".

* * *

After his shift, he and Doctor Julian Bashir walked along the Promenade towards Quark's in their World War Two pilot gear. He'd rather be discussing this with Keiko but she and Molly are down on Bajor and he doesn't want to bother her. Julian, though? He's been regularly unloading about his relationship with the Dabo girl, Miles figures it'd be fair play.

"I can imagine it was disturbing seeing yourself die like that… you did have the appropriate counseling then?"

"Yeah – but it's not quite that – the Miles who died was from this reality, and I replaced him. I can't help but wonder if I'd be as selfless as him, as heroic…"

Julian smiles, kindly.

"But he was you, you are him. However heroic he was, you can be. It's daft to be in awe of the actions of another self. It's not like the Mirror Universe, that Miles and you only diverged by a few hours."

Miles shrugs.

"But what if he had an epiphany? Something that made his sacrifice heartfelt in a way I can't comprehend?" Julian looks sideways at Miles, a little smile- mischievous.

"However, I think you're buried the lead here – did you really say –"

Miles thinks with a weary sigh here we go…

"– Cello?!"

"Yes, I play cello. I was in a quartet on the *Enterprise*. When I was assigned to DS9, there wasn't enough room for it and, anyway…"

"Anyway?" Julian catches his reflection in

a shop window, adjusting the May West floatation vest, smiles to himself approving of his dashing look.

I'm having an existential crisis and he's preening, thinks Miles.

"Keiko's not the biggest fan of it. For the first few months work was non-stop, so I fell out of the habit."

"Playing music can be wonderfully therapeutic. Don't you miss it?"

Miles pauses, shakes his head.

"D'y'know, I don't think I do? Isn't that funny? Me Da made me practice so much as a kid, but I'm so busy with the station I never give it a second thought – I wonder…"

They reached Quark's, Julian gestures for Miles to go ahead of him –

"Well, don't … string me along…"

Miles sighs again.

"How did I end up with you as a friend?"

Julian, now smiling broadly, "Best friend…"

As they entered the bar, Quark stepped out in front of them- beaming with all the sincerity he could fabricate.

"Gentlemen! Here for another of your Holosuite adventures?"

Past him, Miles spotted a group of strangers clustered by the bar, desperately trying not to be noticed. One in particular – a human figure with an ridge across his forehead, seemed to be part of them, yet oddly separate. As he turned, the 'ridge' opened to reveal a third eye, working independently of the other two, looking directly at the Chief. He quickly turned away. Miles was taken aback, but then Quark spoke:

"So! Chief! Doctor! Looking forward to taking on those Nazyites in their flying ships?"

"*Nazis*. In *aeroplanes*. And yes!" The Doctor beamed, a child-like enthusiasm behind his eyes. He climbed the stairs, his focus on the adventure ahead. Miles was aware of the man looking at him (with all three eyes?) curiously, but shook his head. Let Quark have his intrigue, they'd better things to do. And third eye guy? So many races were coming through the Wormhole from the

Gamma Quadrant, it was all Starfleet Exobiology could do to keep up.

He and Julian had planes to fly…

* * *

Aboard a Bristol Blenheim bomber, they were taking major flak as they advanced as part of the air armada on the French coastal city of Dieppe. Swinging his machine gun nest around, Miles was taking out the seemingly endless lines of FW190s that swooped down.

"Jerry's outnumbering us!" yelled Miles, over the hail of gunfire.

Julian, at the controls, banked the huge bomber, avoiding blasts of anti-aircraft explosions, their smoke filling the dawn sky.

"Hold tight, gunner! As soon as the Typhoons and Spitfires take out those heavy artillery positions, we'll be home free!"

Miles swung around, aware of a second flank opening up, of Messerschmitt Bf 109Es cutting through the smoky sky to his right, tracking up the coast. As they approached, one took out a Bristol

Boston Bomber, a wing now aflame as it plunged towards the Channel.

"Bogies at 3 o'Clock!" He opened fire…

… and nothing happened.

Through his canopy he could see the Boston hanging, maybe 50 meters above the water, the 109Es suspended in smoke above and to the side of him. Nothing moved, all silent.

"– The bloody hell?!" he struggled down from his perch atop the vast aeroplane, back within the fuselage. "Hey Julian, has the program –"

He stopped, as he saw in alarm that, like the rest of their holographic 'crew', Julian was inert. Lurched to the side, hands gripping the controls.

"– frozen" he finished, almost redundantly.

He experimentally prodded Julian on the nose.

No response.

"Nope. Nothing." he prodded again, just to be sure.

Miles stood (an awkward proposition as the aeroplane was

"THE MILES WHO DIED WAS FROM THIS REALITY, AND I REPLACED HIM. I CAN'T HELP BUT WONDER IF I'D BE AS SELFLESS AS HIM, AS HEROIC..."

banked at about 30') and raised his voice.

"Computer! End program!" but the plane didn't go away. "Arch!" but no doorway materialized. He inched along the bulkhead, a mess of wires, dials and bucket seats not easy to negotiate in the best of circumstances. He closed his eyes, visualizing the doorway in his mind. He reached out, and felt the access panel. He manually dragged the door open. Nothing electronic was responding.

A strange light poured in, pulsing. Where the heck was that coming from?!

* * *

From the mezzanine, Miles looked down to see the suspicious group from earlier clustered around a box, maybe a meter high. It's front was propped open, overlaying waves of light seeping out, multicolored, streaming and fluctuating. A monotonous low hum accompanied it.

A glance around the bar told Miles that everyone had been rendered inert. Was the box the cause?

Taking the steps two, three, at a time he bounded to the source of this problem. The light was pulsing out stronger now, so bright he couldn't make out what was inside. The sound got louder too: discordant, erratic.

As he approached it, he sensed eyes on him, though everyone was mannequin still.

… Or was it just an eye?

He was suddenly aware of someone in his peripheral vision, and ducked, quickly, as the figure swung at him. Miles was up again and pinning the man against the staircase.

"Oi! Do you bloody mind?!" yelled the Chief. The three-eyed man blinked, first his main eyes, then the third. His expression was one of deep alarm.

"Now, are you going to tell me just what the hell is going on here?"

The man gestured for Miles to

loosen his grip, he did.

"I…" he gasped, recovering his composure "I don't understand! How are you … animate? Are you behind this?!"

Miles' eyes narrowed "I could ask you the same, fella."

The man composed himself. "I'm Commander Ganeri Criss – Starfleet TIC."

Miles looked confused. "TIC? What division is that?"

"It's… not established yet…"

Miles shook his head "So let me guess – the 'T' is for time?"

"Good as. Temporal Integrity Commission. We study and deal with anomalies, leave before creating a paradox… Like this… but it's not stopping… I don't know –"

"Why's everyone here frozen, and what is that –" he gestured towards the glowing box.

He was suddenly aware of a change in the structure of the bar. Was it… aging? *Decaying*?

"– and what's it doing to the bar?!"

MILES PUT HIS HEAD IN HIS HANDS. WAS THIS HOW IT ENDED? DS9, FOR ALL HIS WORK, DESTROYED BY A BUM NOTE?

"We received an alert in the 29th century," Criss replied. "I was sent by temporal transporter to investigate – I arrived 48 hours ago, before –" he paused…

"Before?" asked Miles, it wasn't going to be good…

"Before DS9 disintegrates… *today*."

* * *

Criss looked in the box.

"It appears to be a temporal device –"

"A *bomb?!*" Miles challenged.

Criss shook his head. "No, an artifact of some kind. Your Ferengi bar-owner acquired it from the Gamma Quadrant, and was going to sell it to the highest bidder. I insinuated myself into the group…"

Miles looked around at the skeevy figures by the bar.

"Unfortunately," Criss continued, "opening its case activated it – and now it's accelerating entropy in the bar. Eventually, it will spread to the whole station and DS9'll turn to dust. I wasn't frozen in time, as I'm chronometrically distinct from this time – but you?"

Miles shrugged. "Future version of myself from a parallel reality. I must be just different enough to not be affected…"

Criss pointed to his forehead "That's why my Hi-Eye registered you," he mused "This station and parallel realities… almost as bad as the *Enterprise*!" he paused. "*any Enterprise…*"

"Can I do anything?" Miles asked, looking at the artifact, curiously. "I'm an engineer. Is there some technical solution? Something I can twist, or hit, or calibrate?"

Criss shook his head. The station shuddered around them. The Dabo table was crumbling, cracks appearing through the floor. Not long now.

"No – it's something to do with harmonics, they're discordant, that's what's causing the entropic effect – if only there was a way to regulate them…"

Miles put his head in his hands. Was this how it ended? DS9, for all his work, destroyed by a bum note?

His face changed… a crazy, crazy thought…

"This artifact, can I hold it?"

Criss looked wary. "What good would that do?"

Miles smiled.

* * *

The TIC officer braced the box as Miles struggled to extract the artifact. The floor starting to splinter under their feet, as he desperately kept his balance holding the device.

It was a carved wood structure, an elegant swirl: a helix. It was hollow. Between top and base strands were fixed, crossing the shape. Through the center of the structure was a thin stem. A bow.

Miles smiled again.

Criss looked at it, alarmed "What are you going to do? We can't beam it off the station. Don't you dare break it!"

They lurched as the station shifted, panels falling. Miles held the artifact tightly.

"I'm not going to break it. I'm going to play it."

* * *

Taking the stem, Miles drew it across the 'strings'. The rumbling in the station momentarily quietened. As he paused, the whine keened, and the cracking slowed. Criss looked baffled "What did you do?!"

Miles considered. "It needs regulating, a continuous harmonic sequence," he replied, knowing that whatever he did here would mean life or death for everyone on this station. Thousands depended on his next action. Like that 'other' Miles, this was something he knew he could do, had to do.

He lifted it – it was nothing like a cello but he understood it, instinctively. With one hand pressing strings, the other running the 'bow',

he played. A soaring, beautiful tune – as he arco-ed, his eyes closed, in the moment.

As the tune rose, elegant and fragile on this strange instrument, the entropic effect reversed. The bar became whole once more. On the final dying notes, the light diffused, and other sounds came in –

– the hum of the crowd. Time had started again.

Quark looked at him, shocked "*Chief?!!* How did you get here and what the hell are you playing at?"

Miles smiled. "The Lark Ascending, Vaughan Williams."

Behind them, Criss placed the instrument back in the case. "I'm confiscating this, on Starfleet authority."

Quark blustered. "You can't do that! It's *mine*! I own it! This is an outrage!"

Criss smiled "I'm sure you can show us the appropriate paperwork –"

Quark glowered. Looked at Miles and Criss. Shook his head. Then, disgruntled, beaten, he turned to the group, herding them away. "OK,

show over! Apologies, gentlebeings, please settle your bar bills, this auction is concluded."

Julian came down the stairs "Miles?! Where on Earth did you disappear to?"

"We had an… engineering emergency." he smiled at Criss, who nodded.

Julian looked baffled as Criss tapped a comm-badge. "Thank you, Chief. Keep up the music. No need to report this?"

"Wouldn't know what to write, anyway?" smiled Miles.

He left in a transporter glow, the box with him. Julian, utterly baffled, looking between where the vanishing officer had stood, and Miles.

"What? *What?!*"

Miles squeezed Julian's shoulder. "Let's get back to Dieppe…"

What he didn't tell his friend, what he couldn't express was the epiphany he had as he made the artifact work: that he'd never stopped making music. That DS9 was now his instrument, vast and elegant, and every day he tuned her, finding harmonies and played – made her sing across the stars. ★

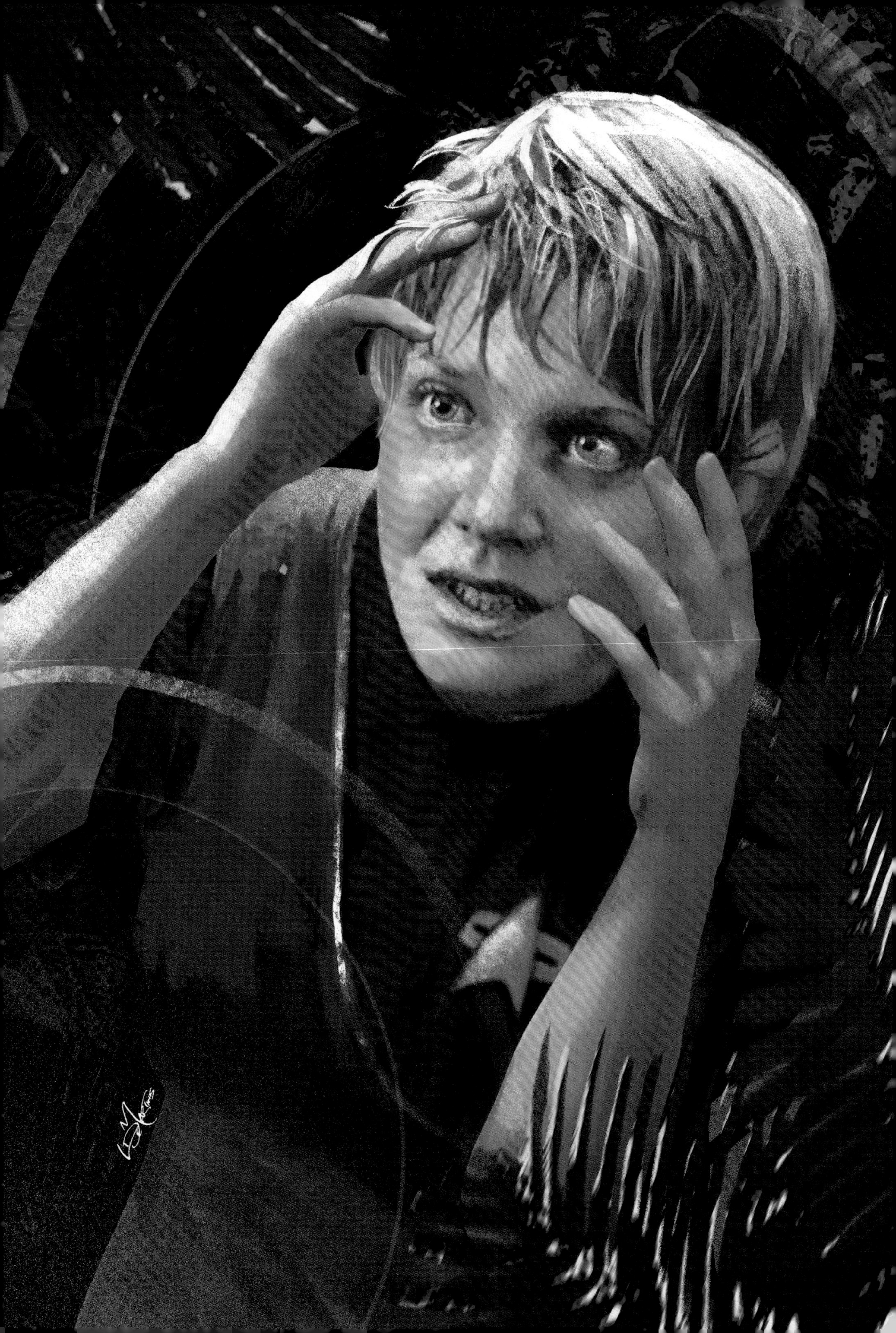

See & Seen

STORY: PETER HOLMSTROM
ILLUSTRATION: LOUIE DE MARTINIS

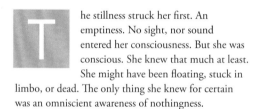

The stillness struck her first. An emptiness. No sight, nor sound entered her consciousness. But she was conscious. She knew that much at least. She might have been floating, stuck in limbo, or dead. The only thing she knew for certain was an omniscient awareness of nothingness.

She was alone.

Her mind went to her youth – the stillness that only a contained underground community could offer, a loving father, and awareness that everything would be provided for. But that was two years ago, and Kes was no longer a child.

Her dreams of seeing the stars had taken her to the starship *U.S.S. Voyager* – determined to traverse the galaxy in search of their home. Growing up around countless new cultures thrilled her with wonder each and every day. Yet she was Ocampan. An alien. An "other."

"Imagine you are listening to a symphony and focusing on a single instrument," Tuvok had said a few days prior while exercising her telepathic abilities. But there was no symphony here, not even a single instrument. Just silence.

With her father's image in her mind, Kes opened her eyes to a world of stars above, dancing around in streaks of purple and white. She had often heard the crew of *Voyager* refer to stars as "specs of white," but never had the nerve to ask what they meant. Stars were always white and purple streaks through her eyes, like dancing fairies against a screen of dreams.

Kes lifted her head to stare around. She was on a planet teaming with life – at least, it should have been. Trees, shrubs, and vines surrounded her, but appeared almost frozen in time. The only movement came from the waving reflection of moonlight, and the streaks of stars above. Stars…

It all came rushing back. *Voyager*, the shuttlecraft mission with Captain Janeway and Lieutenant B'Elanna Torres, the malfunction… the crash. The last thing Kes remembered was B'Elanna preparing to eject the warp core, then she woke up here…

Kes rose to see the wreckage of the shuttle strewn around her. Sparks from flickering consoles as the power surged, then dissipated, added a ghostly sheen to the surroundings. She wiped her hand across her short blonde hair to find it caked with blood. She should be dead. Even if B'Elanna had ejected the core, doing so in an M-class planet's atmosphere would have been catastrophic. They all should be dead. And yet…

In the shadows of the jungle, a movement caught Kes's eyes. She tried to focus, but couldn't be sure if her eyes were deceiving her. The trees stretched away, inward and outward, seemingly at the same time. Kes struggled to keep the visage in her mind, and shook her head. There was something. At least, she thought she saw something… If only Captain--

Kes's mind flew to Captain Janeway. Her eyes darted around to find Janeway and B'Elanna spread out on the wreckage. She scrambled over to Janeway's unconscious body, and checked for a sign of life, remembering the lessons in human anatomy the Doctor had taught her. There was a heartbeat, but it was weak. Kes closed her eyes and reached out with her mind.

Captain, please wake up.

Janeway's muscles shuddered back to awareness, as her eyes fluttered open.

"Kes? What happened? Did you…?" Kes unconsciously recoiled away from Janeway.

"I'm sorry, Captain. You were unconscious and I…" Kes closed her mouth at a loss for words.

A wave of shame crashed over Kes at the thought of her using her telepathic abilities to wake the captain up. It had been only a few short days since *Voyager's* encounter with the Ocampan colony, and one specific Ocampan, Tanis, who helped Kes unlock telekinetic powers beyond her wildest dreams. So alluring was this new power, Kes felt herself fall in love with its potential – addicted to the ecstasy of having power over life and death. But Tanis had been

a liar, and by opening the door of Kes's potential, it nearly cost Tuvok his life. With Tanis's departure, the door to that potential had closed, and her abilities had returned to a benign state. That's what she told herself, anyway.

Ever since that day, she'd felt the stares of the other crew members on her back. Despite the fact that Tuvok had healed, damage repaired, and all was forgiven and forgotten – the stares remained. The eyes, the whispers –

(monster)

-- dogged Kes wherever she went. It frightened her…

"It's all right, Kes." Janeway smiled and reached out her hand to Kes for help, bringing Kes out of her thoughts. "Where's B'Elanna?"

"I'm here. Somehow" the half-Klingon chief engineer barked as she pushed herself to her feet. "This stupid shuttle malfunctioned.

The core didn't eject, so instead of bouncing off the atmosphere into space, we crashed."

"But we're still here, so the matter/anti-matter containment must have held." Janeway stared around and moved towards B'Elanna.

"That shouldn't be possible, Captain. We were venting coolant—"

"--Captain, when I awoke, I—" Kes froze, unable to put into words the mysterious jungle visage.

"Yes?" Janeway stared at her, while B'Elanna shot an impatient glare. Kes always felt like a little girl around the captain, half ashamed, like she had been caught with her hand in the cookie jar.

"It, it might have been nothing—"

"We don't have time for this, Captain." B'Elanna's sharp voice gave Kes a start. "*Voyager* could be on the other side of the quadrant by now."

"Then we have a bit of time, don't we? Kes?"

Kes stared at the two women with wide eyes for a moment.

"It was nothing. Shadows playing tricks."

"Well, glad we've got that taken care of…"

"It's all right, B'Elanna. Kes, if you see anything else, feel free to say so."

Kes's emotions boiled inside of her as she watched Janeway and B'Elanna turn back to the downed shuttlecraft. B'Elanna's impatience was expected, but the Captain?

Sending me back to my room, like a child who cried Kazon.

Kes marched away from the crash and towards the jungle. The vine-like plants glowed with a dark purplish hue reflected off the moonlight. Despite all this vegetation, she still felt nothing around her. But how can that be? Plants do not merely appear from nothing, which means there must be life of some sort. Yet, she felt—

No, it's not that she felt *nothing*, it's that she felt the absence of nothing. As if something was recoiling from her. Hiding from her.

Kes closed her eyes and stretched out with her mind, attempting to visualize, as Tuvok taught her, the inner world of this planet. As she

KES'S EMOTIONS BOILED INSIDE OF HER AS SHE WATCHED JANEWAY AND B'ELANNA TURN BACK TO THE DOWNED SHUTTLECRAFT. B'ELANNA'S IMPATIENCE WAS EXPECTED, BUT THE CAPTAIN?

tried, a sudden impulse overtook her to call for—

"Capt—"

Kes's legs gave out from under her, as if a giant earthquake had pulled the ground away, sending her to the ground. Yet, she had felt no earthquake. Kes looked up to see the jungle was suddenly ablaze with fire.

"Captain!" Kes turned, but neither Janeway nor B'Elanna seemed to notice anything. "Captain!" Finally, they looked up and rushed over.

"Kes, what's wrong?"

"The fir –" Kes turned, but the jungle had returned to normal. "Captain, there was a fire. The jungle was ablaze." B'Elanna pulled out her tricorder and scanned.

"There's no evidence of a fire."

"I wasn't mistaken. I saw it." Janeway kneeled to help Kes to her feet.

"I believe you, Kes. Perhaps the moonlight is playing tricks."

Janeway placed a tender hand on

Kes's shoulder, but she barely felt it.

Kes remained where she stood as Janeway and B'Elanna returned to the downed shuttlecraft. She looked up to the moon, steeped in an orangish hue against a purple sky, and she wondered if perhaps –

"Do… think… coincidence, Captain?" Kes barely heard B'Elanna's whispers. She leaned over in the direction of the two women and strained her elongated ears to try and hear more.

"She burns through the hydroponics bay, nearly kills Tuvok, and now she sees fires everywhere."

"You think she's still carrying the trauma of her telekinetic explosions?" Janeway mused.

"I think we—

(monster)

-- might need to consider that she's creating these fires herself. The shuttle should not have crashed, Captain. Kes might not even know what she's doing."

Janeway rubbed her forehead.

"I will not engage in this witch hunt level mentality. Not until we get more data." Janeway continued, but Kes stopped listening, turning away towards the jungle.

She could feel the tears moments away from bursting forth. The jungle fire, the emptiness around her, Tuvok, Tanis, the hydroponics bay… Perhaps she really was losing her mind…

A movement in the jungle caught Kes's eye. A vine-like tree swayed violently back and forth. Then another next to it. Then another. Soon, every tree surrounding the crash site whipped to and fro as if a surge of wind drove them. Yet, there was no wind.

"Kes!" Janeway rushed towards her.

"You see it too?!" Kes could barely hear her own voice over the barrage of sounds from the trees encircling them.

"Kes, stop this!" B'Elanna barked.

"This isn't me!"

Janeway placed a protective arm around her. "We have no evidence this is coming from Kes. Stand down, Lieutenant."

B'Elanna pulled out her tricorder and shoved the results toward Janeway. "We have no evidence of anything, Captain! This isn't technically happening!"

"There has to be evidence of something! I will not believe Kes is the cause of this!"

Kes pushed Janeway's arm away.

"I don't need your protection, Captain." Kes stared back and forth between Janeway and B'Elanna – a combination of fear and compassion on Janeway's face. "I am not a monster!"

Janeway's shoulders sank, her eyes focused on Kes's, as if none of the madness around them existed.

"Kes… We do not blame you for what happened."

"I've seen the way they look at me! The way she looks at me!" B'Elanna turned away, in a movement as close as her Klingon blood would allow for shame.

"Some do react with fear or aggression at things they don't understand. But we don't turn people

away for who they are – we learn and marvel at our differences. Forever in awe of what could be. You're a part of our crew, Kes. We wouldn't turn our backs on you." Janeway had inched forward enough to where her arms nearly touched Kes's. Kes closed the distance to embrace Janeway as tight as she could.

A fresh burst of movement crashed through the trees. Kes parted from Janeway's embrace to stare towards the jungle.

"Perhaps— B'Elanna!"

Kes turned to see B'Elanna now on the ground, writhing in pain. Her body was slowly disintegrating. Janeway was kneeling beside her, staring in horror.

Janeway crooked her head towards Kes with a look of concentrated malevolence.

"You did this!"

"No. I told you, this wasn't me!"

"You killed us!"

"No!" Kes closed her eyes from the scene, could not believe what she was seeing.

Would not.

"This isn't real! The Captain would never say this to me! Ne—"

"Kes?!"

Kes opened her eyes. She was on the ground, seated with her back to the shuttlecraft wreckage. Janeway stroked Kes's cheek with concern.

"Are you all right?"

"Yes, I—B'Elanna!" Kes reached out to the alive B'Elanna crouched beside Janeway.

B'Elanna lightly pushed Kes's arm away from her. "We still have a situation here." The trees thrashed as Kes had never seen. Almost as if they were--

"Captain, I believe I know what's going on."

Janeway looked at Kes with suspicion. "Anything you can point to scientifically?"

Kes shook her head. "No. I… need to go into the jungle."

"The hell you do," B'Elanna retorted.

"Captain, I have to do this." Janeway stared out to the jungle, then back to Kes.

"I'm sorry, Kes. I can't—"

Kes broke away from Janeway's hands and rushed towards the jungle.

"Kes, come back!" Janeway ran after Kes, but as she did so, the thrashing of the trees intensified to the point that she could no longer follow. It was as if the jungle itself wanted Kes to come alone.

Vines and foliage parted before Kes as she ran, engulfing and sealing her in as she moved deeper and deeper, until finally she came to a small clearing.

"I'm here!" She cried out to the void. "What do you want to tell me?"

The trees stopped moving, and an eerie silence encased the clearing. Kes's mind went back to her childhood. The feeling of her father's embrace, and the protection she felt. The fear struck her again – the loneliness, the monster that may lie within her.

"Do not fear your negative thoughts. They are part of you. They are a part of every living being. To pretend it does not exist is to create an opportunity for it to escape." Tuvok's words from their previous lesson rang in her ears. Kes took a breath, and for the first time since her last encounter with Tanis, she pushed at the door to her potential.

I'm here. Can you understand me?
Plant life from all around her

"SHE BURNS THROUGH THE HYDROPONICS BAY, NEARLY KILLS TUVOK, AND NOW SHE SEES FIRES EVERYWHERE."

shuddered, exerting a powder-like substance from within. The powder floated down towards Kes, as if guided by a single force. The powder took shape, growing, bending, until it formed the hollow image of a humanoid, suspended in the air with neither mass nor form, defying all Kes had ever seen.

Can you speak to me? Kes could only hope her words found a home. The figure raised its "hand" towards her. Kes approached, and let the hand rest on her forehead.

A wave of images flooded her mind -- images she could barely understand, barely comprehend, until...

I understand.

A tear dripped down Kes's face.

I'm sorry…

"It's really quite simple," the

Doctor smugly explained. "Kes's Ocampan physiology has perception quite different to humans or Klingons, making her attuned to the alien's visual wave-length. I could have deduced that in moments…"

Two days had passed since Kes's encounter in the Jungle with the alien being called the Anoallidin. *Voyager* had only just rescued them, after B'Elanna established communications. The Doctor continued to scan Janeway and B'Elanna, as Kes stared on.

"There's still one thing I don't understand," Janeway mused. "If 'Anoallidin' viewed our crash as an attack, why save our lives? Why not just let us die in the explosions?"

"The planet we crashed on was not a collection of lifeforms, but one lifeform spread amongst

millions of… cells. That's why our scans revealed nothing – they had no framework for understanding such a lifeform. I believe Anoallidin couldn't comprehend seeing life end, no more than it could comprehend having its life endangered.

"They could've just said hello," B'Elanna snorted.

"The Anoallidin communicate through images as opposed to words. Meaning doesn't come from association but from reference. The trees, my visions, it was all to say we were hurting it by our leaking coolant during the crash."

"Remarkable," Janeway got up and placed her hands on Kes's shoulders. "And Kes, I hope you're alright."

"Yes, Captain." Kes smiled. "You were right. There is so much to be in awe of." ⋆

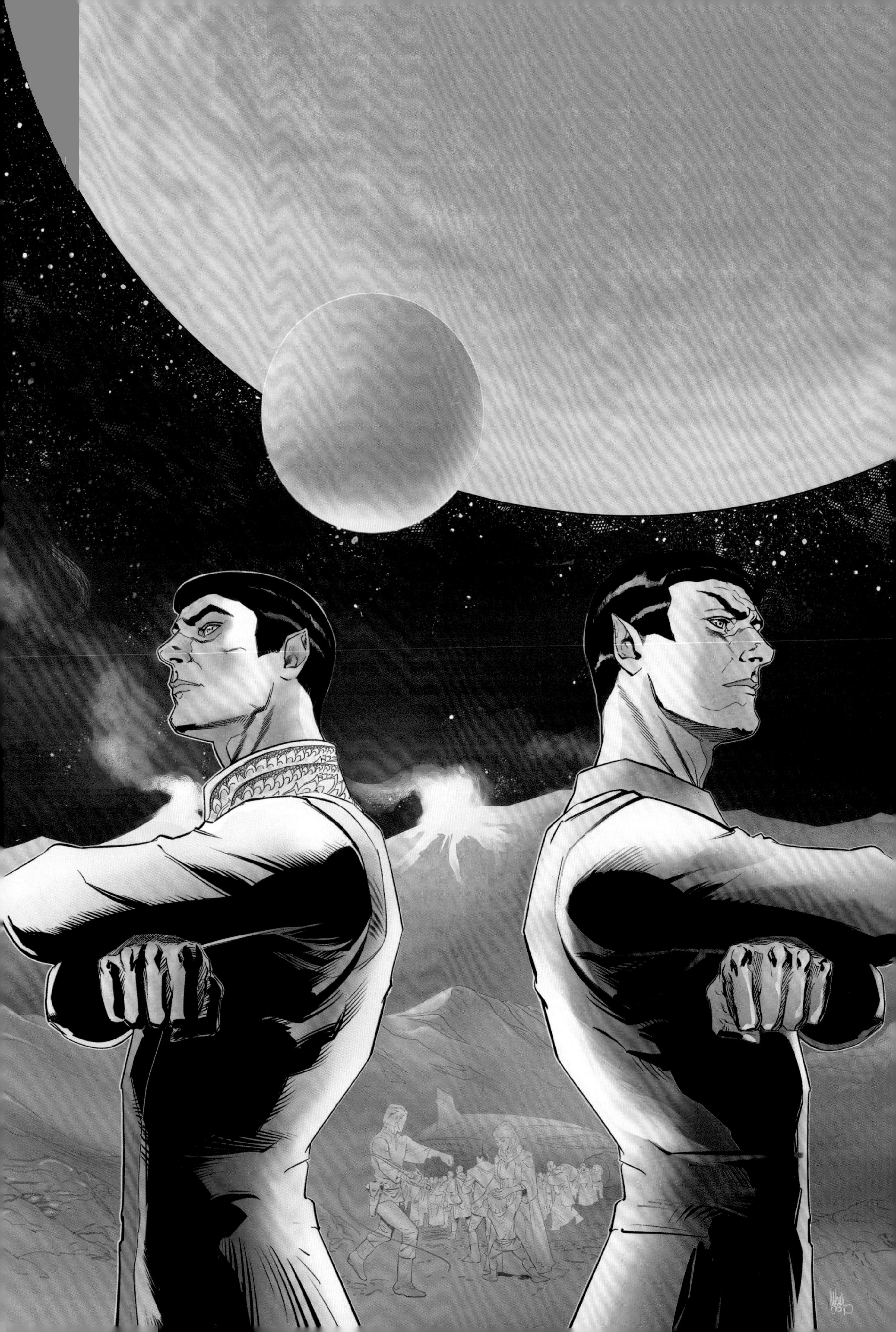

Sundering

STORY: DAVID MACK
ILLUSTRATION: WAMBERTO NICOMEDES

VULCAN
421 C.E. (Earth Calendar)

o many lives wasted, Suvok lamented. *So much destruction.*

The mathematician squinted to guard his eyes from a searing wind laced with radioactive dust. Deadly gusts plagued the surface of Vulcan, and would do so for decades to come – just one consequence of a world ravaged by decades of civil war. To the south, the ruined city of K'lan-ne spewed black smoke into the ruddy morning sky. It and dozens more cities had been left to smolder like the ancient grudges Suvok blamed for their annihilation.

Steep is the price of ignorance wedded to pride and anger.

Memories of Vulcan's brutal civil war evoked intense emotions for Suvok. During the war he had found it a challenge to hold fast to the teachings of Surak; controlling his reactions in the face of wanton savagery had tested his hard-won mental discipline, but the future of his world and people had depended upon it.

A culture ravaged by passion devoid of reason would be one doomed to self-extermination – as would be one that failed to expunge itself of toxic elements. Consequently, with this breaking dawn, the exodus of Vulcan's irrational ones had begun.

A strong desert breeze fluttered Suvok's robes and tousled his short hair but had no effect on the wrapped garment or braided coiffure of his wife, L'Naal. She had been stoic and unwavering in her support of all he had done to end Vulcan's civil war

while there was still something of their world and culture to be salvaged from its cinders. At their feet sat their year-old son, Kevok. He had Suvok's features but L'Naal's hair, and his complexion was a compromise between his father's pale skin with olive undertones and his mother's rich umber skin.

Too young yet for language or appreciation of anything beyond his own immediate needs, Kevok had no understanding of the events transpiring around him. Suvok suppressed a momentary pang of envy of his son's lack of conscious awareness. There would be many – himself among them – who would later wish they could excise from their minds the memory of this somber day.

For several kilometers to either side of Suvok and his kin stood more people than Suvok could easily count. Families, couples, and individuals had gathered along the length of a tall barrier of wire mesh topped with sharp coils. It ran parallel to the contours of the northwest shore of the island continent of Xir'tan, with guarded gates located every few kilometers along its span.

On the other side of the barrier, the sea tore itself into ragged blankets of foam with each wave that crashed upon the rocky shore. On the sand, just beyond the reach of the high tide, hundreds of interstellar colony-transport ships stood parked like great leviathans of the deep.

Crowding the narrow strip of beach between the transports and the wire-mesh barrier were tens of thousands of people who had been sentenced to permanent exile for swearing allegiance to anarchy rather than order. Cast out with them were entire families, including adolescents and young children. Every one of them banished in the name of Logic and Reason.

Suvok watched exiles straggle past on the other side of the fence. He eyed their ragged, weary ranks and hoped he had not come too late. None of Vulcan's outcasts returned his attention. In defiance of Surak's profound and liberating dictums of logic, the apostates were awash in emotions. Visages clenched in rage traveled beside those drawn in fear or contorted by sorrow. Their ranks susurrated with vows of revenge and sobs of regret. Tears fell only to be swallowed by the sand, or trampled beneath the procession of shuffling feet.

From amid the legion of dusty faces, Suvok found the one he sought, the one he knew as well as his own, because in a sense it *was* his own. Suvok's identical twin brother Sokor held his wife, T'Vala, close to his side. Her long black hair, now dirty and tangled, danced in the ceaseless wind while she cradled their baby daughter, Taavik, in her bare, scarred arms.

They all seemed oblivious of Suvok and his family until he called to them a second time: "Sokor! T'Vala! Wait!"

Sokor and T'Vala stopped and faced Suvok. Dressed in filthy tatters and scraps, they looked as if they had been dredged from the depths of a nightmare. Other exiles coursed past them like a slow river. The young couple forded the sluggish current of the dispossessed on their way to the fence. By the time they stood on the other side of the barrier from Suvok and L'Naal, they had changed their expressions from blank masks into portraits of contempt.

Sokor bristled with resentment. "Come to gloat, Suvok?"

The accusation would have been insulting coming from anyone, but Suvok found it galling coming from his twin. "A most illogical query, brother. Nothing would be gained by indulging such a selfish emotion."

The angry young poet clenched his hands into fists. "If I could reach through this fence, I'd show you how satisfying a negative emotion can be. For *one* of us, anyway."

"I did not come to prolong our conflict, Sokor."

"Then why are you here? Did you come to say you're sorry you sided with authoritarians who banished us for no greater crime than existing as nature made us? Or maybe you came to witness our expulsion in person so you can rest assured that you've finished what you started."

"It was not the disciples of Surak who instigated this conflict, brother. It was your own agents of anarchy who first resorted to violence. Who chose to topple our cities and set our world aflame rather than accept our only viable road to peace."

"*Your* only road to peace. The rest of us should not have to suffer because your ilk lacks the will to master your passions by any means short of psychological castration."

"We who put aside emotion and embrace logic should not have to risk the extinction of our species and the destruction of our world because your kind are too weak or too selfish to overcome the primitive aspects of our shared nature, in the name of the common good."

Sokor shook his head. "There is no *common good*. Not any more. There is only what is good for *us*, and what is good for *you*." He glanced over his shoulder at the transport ships. "But the fact that you're putting millions of us onto ships and launching us into deep space with no preset destination betrays the lie behind your logic. You've won the war. Taken our weapons and our homes. Corralled us into camps. Sentenced us to exile." He clenched the wire mesh of the fence between them. "But even now, you're still afraid of us. For all your talk of logic, your path to peace is paved with *fear*."

* * *

L'Naal was unwilling to remain silent any longer. "It is not fear of what you represent that led to your kind's expulsion, Sokor. It is a rational desire for stability. Order. Peace."

Her interjection stoked Sokor's temper. "You speak of those things as if they are unique to the followers of Surak and alien to his critics. Such sophistry is beneath you, L'Naal."

"It is not sophistry to conclude one cannot trust compacts made with those who reject reason and logic. Your self-interest is driven by factors beyond the rational. You let your pride and your resentments color your decision-

A CULTURE RAVAGED BY PASSION DEVOID OF REASON WOULD BE ONE DOOMED TO SELF-EXTERMINATION...

making. That is a recipe for bad-faith negotiation and, as your confederates have demonstrated, betrayal."

Sokor's wife, T'Vala, put herself between him and L'Naal. It was a telling action; it suggested to L'Naal that her argument had provoked the woman to the point that she felt it necessary to defend her mate physically as well as rhetorically. "Do you hear yourself, L'Naal? You invoke logic as if it were a totem against suffering and the only foundation upon which trust can be built. But *trust* is never about logic, it is about *faith*."

L'Naal folded her hands together in front of her waist. "No loyalty is perfect, T'Vala. But an agreement grounded in logic accounts for rational self-interest and takes into account a need for equitable balance and accountability. None of which your kind can be trusted to respect. Need I remind you it was *your* side that made the unilateral decision to escalate our philosophical disagreement into war

by committing grievous acts of lethal violence and mass destruction?"

Before T'Vala could answer, Sokor edged in front of her to confront L'Naal. "No, it was you and the other zealots of Surak who fired the figurative first shot of this conflict, when you condemned all who did not blindly accept your cold-hearted prophet's call to reject thousands of years of our history and traditions, in order to forge a future of *bland conformity*."

* * *

"Not conformity, brother – *unity*." Suvok saw his twin's hands curl into fists. Rather than mirror him, Suvok focused on his sense of calm and balance. "Without a unifying philosophy, our civilization was trapped in an endless cycle of struggle. Our conflict perpetuated itself for its own sake, just as a flame seeks fuel to sustain its burning. For the survival of our species, Sokor, we must break the

cycle – or else be consumed by it."

Sokor's features hardened with anger and resentment. "Noble words from one whose ideology gets to flourish – while mine is forced to scrape for survival, pilgrims cast out without a plan, left to fend for themselves while they wander the cosmic darkness."

"There are other habitable worlds, brother. Many within a decade's travel. You and those who share your ethos will find the right one to colonize. You will rebuild – and live freely."

"But we will always know we were refugees. As will our offspring, and theirs after them. We will never forget that Surak's children banished us from our ancestral home."

"What would you have had us do instead, Sokor?"

"We could have kept this continent and surrendered the other two to your control."

Suvok had heard that idea before. "Such a peace would not last. Proximity

would invite contact, and contact would reignite the conflict. We need to be one world, one people, one law. To rebuild and advance, we must overcome our biology, and our history."

T'Vala fixed Suvok with a glare as unforgiving as the fires of Vulcan's Forge. "You profess to accept and celebrate an infinite diversity of life and ideas – all except *ours*. And when it comes to your own true nature, you live in denial."

"Not denial, T'Vala – *mastery*."

Her voice darkened with contempt. "You are masters of nothing but lies. You preach pacifism but continue to practice arts of war. You extol the virtue of logic devoid of passion even as the fires of our blood burn within you. You claim to venerate the arts, but you cut yourselves off from the true wellsprings of inspiration."

L'Naal struck a pose of cool defiance. "Our mutual history is one of savage violence, T'Vala. Cruelty. Mayhem. Left unchecked, our passions would have led us into extinction. The path of Surak is our way to a better, sustainable future."

Sokor's anger withered into disappointment. "You see the evils of our past, but not the virtues. Yes, we were violent – but we were also tender. We were capable of cruelty, but we had an equal capacity for kindness. We

"SURAK'S WAY ROBS YOU OF THE BEST PARTS OF YOURSELVES TO SAVE YOU FROM THE WORST – AND BY TAKING EVERYTHING, IT LEAVES YOU EMPTY."

were chaotic, but also spontaneous. *Imaginative.*

"Surak's way robs you of the *best* parts of yourselves to save you from the worst – and by taking everything, it leaves you empty. Tell me, brother: What is the point of a life lived without joy? Without love?"

Suvok replied, "What is the value of a life lived in constant fear of violence, injustice, and suffering? Our passions must be mastered if our society is to thrive."

"Mastered, yes, but not crushed! Not denied! Not suppressed to the point of self-harm. Don't you see what your ethos has done to you? Done to our world?" He gestured toward T'Vala and Taavik. "To *us?* You've won the war – but can't you see what you've *lost?* If you would let yourself *feel* this moment, really feel it, would you be so quick to sanction putting millions of fellow Vulcans onto prison ships? Could you still be so callous that you

could banish your own twin brother and not shed a single tear of regret?"

Suvok weighed his words with care. "I do not deny the existence of my emotions. They are still there, as powerful as they ever were. But I embraced Surak's teachings so that I could master my own mind, and act out of reason for the greater good rather than out of passion to serve my own desires. I have lost nothing of myself, brother. What I have gained is the serenity of reason."

"Wrong. You've lost more than you know – starting with me, your only brother. As for what you've gained? Many years from now, this moment will become a memory that haunts you. You and your fellow travelers are like primitive surgeons hacking at a patient with stone tools. To save the Vulcan body politic … you've torn out its heart."

* * *

Sirens keened and echoed; the launch of the transport ships was only minutes away. On Sokor's side of the fence, armed guards approached to take him, T'Vala, and Taavik to their assigned vessel. Suvok and L'Naal looked back at Sokor and his family through the mesh, their visages blank and cold. It was like staring into the gears of a machine and expecting to find pity.

Tears fell from Sokor's eyes as he made a final effort to elicit a response from his twin. "They're coming for us, Suvok. Coming to haul us away like garbage."

Suvok arched an eyebrow. "Your situation is dire enough that exaggeration seems unnecessary."

"And yet you *do* nothing. *Feel* nothing. *Say* nothing to help us, or comfort us, or even tell us you care what is happening."

"Your side chose war and lost. Now the consequences come due. What more is there to say?"

"That we're still family? That you wish it hadn't come to this?"

"The desires of one individual are irrelevant at times such as this. Whatever I might consider to be a more desirable outcome no longer matters. This is the world we have made, brother."

A guard wearing an emblem of Surak set his hand on T'Vala's shoulder. Another grasped Sokor's arm. Sokor heard other soldiers behind him. There was nothing to be gained from resisting now; even without the benefit of Surakian logical education, he knew that to be true. Tears in Sokor's eyes softened his brother's uncaring image. "Good-bye, Suvok."

"Good-bye, Sokor."

The guards pulled Sokor and T'Vala toward the transports – and then they stopped. They, as well as Suvok and L'Naal, all looked toward the bottom of the fence.

Taavik and Kevok stood facing each other, both pressed against the wire barrier. The toddler cousins had each snaked a couple of tiny digits through gaps in the mesh and entwined them with the other's. Locked together, the children looked into each other's eyes with the far-seeing focus of touch-telepaths who had just forged their first instinctual mind-meld.

A third guard took hold of Taavik and tried to pull her away from the fence.

Taavik and Kevok each tightened their hold on the other's fingers. The guard pulled harder. Taavik shrieked in defiant rage and refused to let go.

In that moment when everyone's eyes were on his and T'Vala's willful daughter, Sokor chanced to note his brother's reaction. It was momentary, the very definition of ephemeral, but Sokor was certain he saw Suvok's emotionless façade slip to betray an upswell of pity and sorrow at the sight of their children fighting so valiantly to resist this cruel and arbitrary sundering. For just that fleeting instant, Sokor was certain he saw the shimmer of tears in Suvok's eyes.

Sokor brushed the guard's hand from his arm and stepped toward the one wrestling in vain with his daughter. "Stop. You're scaring her. Let me help."

The guard at the fence released Taavik and stepped back to make way for Sokor. He kneeled beside his daughter and whispered to her.

"No more tears, Taavik. Say good-bye to Kevok. It's time to go."

Reluctantly, Taavik and Kevok disentangled their fingers. Sokor picked up his daughter and nodded at T'Vala. They fell in behind the guards who led them to their assigned transport ship. As they walked, Taavik perched with teary eyes on Sokor's shoulder, facing backward toward the life and world from which they were being expelled.

Sokor stole a final glance over his shoulder at his kin. Suvok and L'Naal stood together, faces downcast, as if they could not bring themselves to bear witness. But their son Kevok remained at the fence, hands pressed to the wire, his gaze locked inextricably with Taavik's.

Hot winds whipped up funnels of dust that roamed the beach dunes. Climbing the ramp into a transport ship, Sokor knew his people had an arduous journey ahead of them, one they would not all survive. He suspected his descendants and those of the disciples of Surak would meet again someday, most likely as enemies, to reignite this pointless struggle anew.

If only we could learn from our mistakes rather than repeating them, he lamented.

As the transport's engines rumbled, Sokor pulled T'Vala close so they could hug Taavik between them. Looking into his daughter's tear-stained eyes, and remembering how adamantly she and Kevok had clung to each other, Sokor dared to hope there might come a day when the scorned orphans of Vulcan would be welcomed home and called family once more.

My brother would call such hope illogical. Maybe someday he'll understand … hope always is. ★

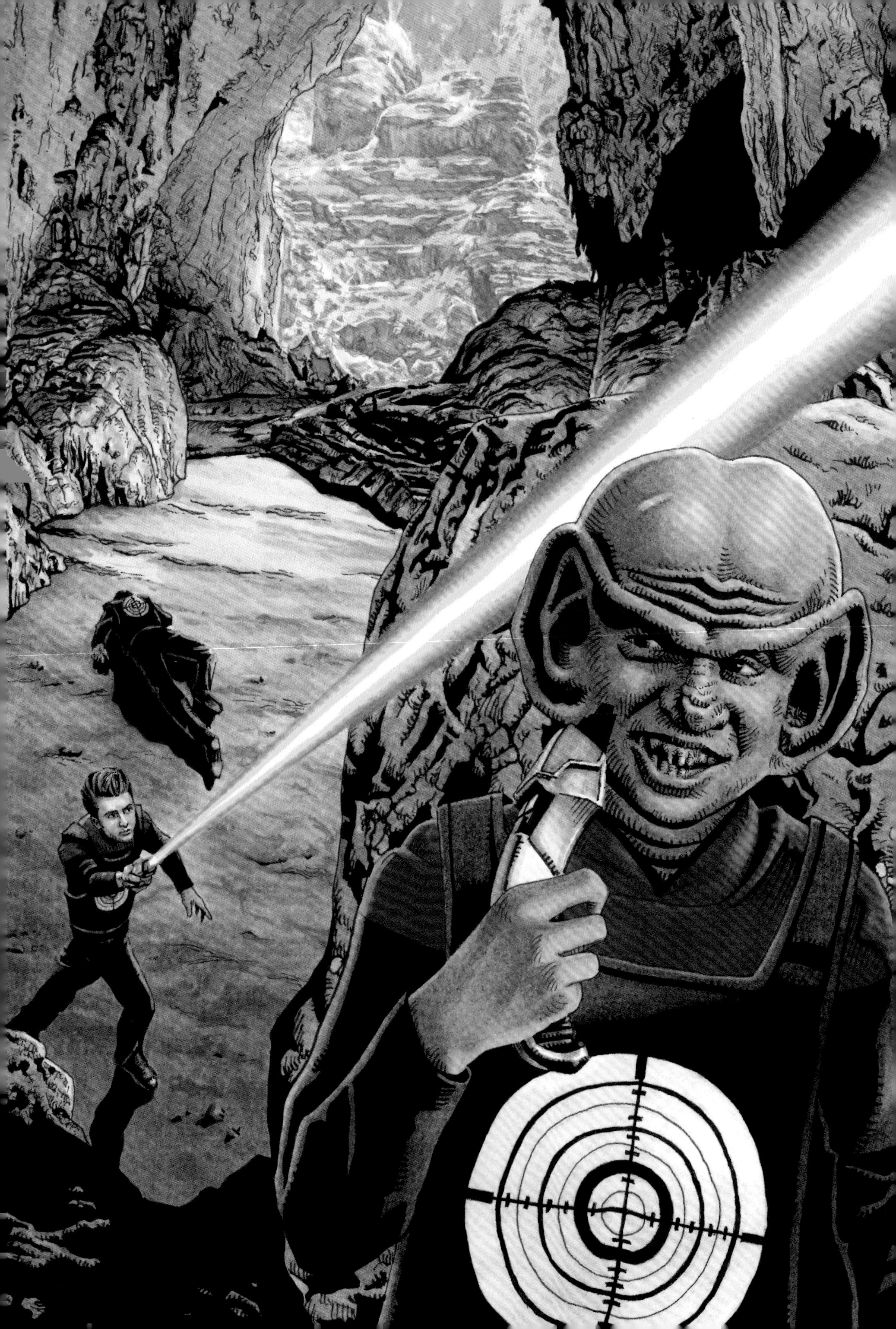

Academy Acquisition

STORY: JAKE BLACK
ILLUSTRATION: ANDY WALKER

lass dismissal tone rang out, and a group of first year cadets exited to the beautiful grounds of Starfleet Academy. It was a perfect day in San Francisco, the sun shining down on the well-manicured grass and trees, birds chirping, and the cadets laughing and having a good time.

All of them, except the Ferengi, Nog, who was trailing behind his classmates.

Nog had found the first weeks at the Academy to be a difficult adjustment compared to life on Deep Space 9. For one thing, he was the only Ferengi on Earth – a fact his fellow cadets rarely let him forget. For another, classes were harder than he'd expected – but he was determined to make it through the Academy and achieve his dream of becoming a decorated officer, making friends along the way.

"Hey! Wait up!" Nog called out, picking up his pace, drawing the attention of some of the cadets.

"What do you want, Nog?" an annoyed Andorian named Schenck asked.

"Anybody want to study with me for Lt. Commander Dillon's xenobiology class later?"

Most of the group scoffed at the offer, but Cadet Whitaker, a human woman, crouched to be eye-to-eye with the Ferengi.

"I might be able to," Whitaker said.

Nog grinned, hopeful that he'd found his first friend. "Really?"

Schenck stepped forward, pulling Whitaker to her feet.

"He just wants to cheat off your homework," Schenck said. "It's what *they* do."

"I would *never* – " Nog began to protest, angrily, but Schenck stepped toward him, pointing at the Ferengi, as if he was in a court room.

"Yeah, right," Schenck countered. "What's that saying your people have? 'You can't free a fish from water'?" Then he turned, and pulled Whitaker away..

Devastated, Nog walked slowly back to his quarters.

Maybe Uncle Quark was right, he thought. *Maybe this was a huge mistake.*

* * *

A short time later, Nog hoped to find some respite from the crushing experience he'd had with his classmates. Struggling to get to sleep, his eyes getting heavy, he lay on his bunk, staring at the ceiling, replaying the incident with Whitaker and Schenck over and over in his mind.

Why are they so cruel? He wondered.

Starfleet was supposed to represent the best of the best and be infinitely inclusive. But so far, Nog knew, Deep Space 9, with all its conflict and danger, ironically seemed to be more welcoming than Starfleet Academy.

Sleep was approaching, yet he still couldn't shake the awful experience he'd just had. Then, as he was about to drift off, a computer voice rang out.

"Priority message for Cadet Nog," the computer

said.

Nog was startled fully awake. He moved to his personal terminal. Who would send him a priority message? Captain Sisko? His father Rom?

"Computer, open message, authorization code Nog Gamma 7-9-9-7," he said.

The screen flashed four simple words from an anonymous sender: "Go back to Ferenginar." Nog buried his head in his hands. He had, in fact, made a terrible mistake.

*   *   *

"Cadets, in seven days you will face your first test in close quarters combat," Academy Tactical Instructor Commander Runnels said. "You will each be issued a point-five type phaser and a targeting sensor vest. You will be placed in a cave-like holodeck simulation. If your sensor is hit by phaser fire, you will be eliminated and removed from the simulation. The last cadet standing will receive the highest marks on the exam."

Nog looked around at his classmates, listening. They were anxious about the test.

"I've never even touched a phaser!"

"I heard that cave simulation is brutal."

"That's why they call Runnels the 'Starfleet Nightmare.'"

"It's going to be great!" Nog exclaimed, silencing the room. Every eye in class focused their full attention on him.

"I mean, it will maybe be great," Nog stammered nervously.

"It is not logical that, for you, it 'will be great,'" a Vulcan named J'Nas said. "Your size and speed will make you an easy target for the rest of us."

"An easy target…" Nog muttered to himself.

*   *   *

Nog sat on a bench on the Academy grounds, reading over Commander Runnels' phaser tactics report on his PADD. In the distance, his sensitive hearing picked up a conversation between a couple of his classmates, Cadets Ford and Thompson.

"This combat test is going to be our ticket to Red Squad," Ford said.

"Absolutely. You up for another practice round tonight?" Thompson replied.

The words "practice round" piqued Nog's interest. He liked Ford and Thompson. Two of the most popular cadets in their class, he felt like they could be his friends. And if they were getting in some practice….

Nog chased down Ford and Thompson, "Hey guys! I hope you don't mind, I overheard you talking about the combat test."

"You overheard?" Ford asked.

Nog motioned to his ears. "Of course. The seventh Rule of Acquisition: 'Keep your ears open.' What's that about some extra practice tonight? Do you mind if I join in? I could *really* use it!"

Ford and Thompson looked at each other and smiled.

"Sure, you can train with us," Thompson said, with a laugh.

"And can you tell me about Red Squad?" Nog continued.

"Of course," Cadet Ford said, causing the Ferengi's eyes to get wide. "Red Squad is the most elite group the Academy has to offer. I'm sure you could get in."

Nog's eyes grew wide, "Wow, really?"

"Oh, for sure! I mean all you'd have to do is buy your way in with latinum. That's how you Ferengi ever do anything, right? Buying opportunity?" Thompson said, his smile turning to a sneer. "That's how you got into the Academy, right?"

Nog's heart fell into his stomach. "That's not fair," he said.

"Well, life's not fair," Ford replied. "By the way, did you get my message the other night?"

Ford and Thompson walked away, laughing.

"THE BIGGER THE SMILE, THE SHARPER THE KNIFE," NOG MUTTERED, HIS VOICE CRACKING.

"The bigger the smile, the sharper the knife," Nog muttered, his voice cracking.

Nog slumped down beneath a large elm tree and began to cry. And then he cried harder. And harder. It was clear he was going to let everyone down. His father, Captain Sisko, even Uncle Quark. And it seemed like his fellow cadets refused to see him as anything other than a stereotype. Tears cut a path down his cheeks, dripping to the ground.

"If you're going to water that tree, best not to use salt water," a man's voice said from above Nog.

Nog rubbed his eyes, wiping the moisture from them with his sleeve, "What?"

"Your tears. The salt in them will kill this tree, and I can't have that. It has to live for another thousand years, at least!" the man said impatiently.

"Who are you?" Nog asked.

"I'm Boothby, the groundskeeper here."

"Well, leave me alone, Boothby," Nog returned, shoulders slumped. He was not in the mood for company.

Nodding, Boothby began pulling weeds in a nearby flowerbed. Nog watched in a mix of curiosity and frustration, as the masterful groundskeeper tended to his work. It was a fascinating display; an odd mix of aggression and care.

"Nog, come here and help me a minute," Boothby asked, motioning to Nog toward him with his trowel, though not looking at him, too focused on the noxious plants sprouting between to his prized flowers.

"How did you…" Nog began. "Oh, right. The token Ferengi. The word's spread, then. Are you going to insult me, too?"

Boothby ignored the question, instead handing Nog a small handheld rake. "Drag this through the soil over here. You'll feel some resistance. That's the weeds' roots. Keep pulling them with the rake until they surface."

Nog obediently followed the groundskeeper's instructions, tugging on clusters of roots beneath the soil. He could feel the roots break, causing them to rise through the soil.

"I don't have time for this. I need to prepare for a combat test," Nog complained. Again, Boothby ignored the comment, gathering the roots Nog had dug up and setting them aside.

"Now, take this and dig some small holes in the dirt where the roots were," Boothby said, handing Nog the trowel.

Nog, again, did as he was asked. Boothby nodded approvingly and filled each hole with seeds.

"We can send signals across

you might be the first Ferengi in Starfleet, but don't let yourself be the last."

"Thank you, Boothby," Nog whispered.

"It's the advantage of a long tail view of all this," Boothby said before leaving Nog for another of his flowerbeds.

* * *

That night, Nog felt the weight of Boothby's words.

I've never been ashamed of being a Ferengi, he thought. *Why should I be? My ears, my size, they* are *assets. They're the best part of me.*

He glanced at the flower Boothby had given him, feeling his confidence grow. *I am going to bloom*! He thought. *And generations of Ferengi will, too.*

* * *

Clad in their target vests, phasers in hand, Nog and his classmates entered the training holodeck. A sprawling cave stood before them. The combatants had 90 seconds to find their initial positions. Nog stood behind a corner on the west side of the cave.

Holding his phaser at the ready, Nog could hear footsteps approaching a long distance away. It was obvious the individual was trying to tip-toe toward his hiding spot. Nog swung around the corner, firing a blast that hit Cadet Schenck directly on his targeting sensor.

"How did you –" he started to say.

"It's what I do!" Nog gleefully replied.

Phaser fire was everywhere! Nog heard targets beep their *Hit* notification and fellow cadets complaining about losing. He couldn't help but laugh when he heard Ford eliminate Thompson.

From a platform above, J'Nas fired toward Nog, who dodged the blast by rolling inside a tiny crevasse in the cave wall. From his protected location, he fired his red beam at J'Nas, eliminating the Vulcan.

Soon, Nog and Ford were the final cadets in the exercise. They exchanged countless blasts of phaser

time and space, deconstruct and reconstruct matter, but we can't have weed-free flowerbeds," Boothby said. "And every few years, we have to replant the seeds for new flowers to grow in place of the weeds."

"Boothby, I really need to…" Nog began.

"You know, you're not the only cadet to ever experience what you are going through," Boothby interrupted curtly. Nog stared at him quizzingly.

"What do you –?"

Boothby patted the soil over the seeds and looked Nog in the eye. "The first member of every species to join Starfleet faces the same suspicion and doubt from their fellow cadets."

Boothby cleaned up the excess dirt and weeds as he continued, "You know Commander Worf? He was the first Klingon. Imagine what he went through thanks to centuries of conflict between the Federation and the Empire."

Nog was caught off guard by Boothby's comment. Though he hadn't gotten to know Worf very well before leaving the station for the Academy, he deeply respected him. He'd never considered what his

Academy experience must have been like.

Nog looked on, lost in thought, as Boothby carefully placed more seeds into the ground. "Not even having his adoptive human brother here prevented him from being bullied."

"That's unbelievable. Who would be foolish enough to pick a fight with *Worf*?"

"Fools is the right word," Boothby said, looking up from his plants and meeting Nog's gaze for the first time. "Only fools bully you, Nog."

"It certainly doesn't feel like that," Nog said quietly.

"You've just been planted in the soil, Nog. But soon, you're going to bloom into something beautiful," Boothby said, pointing first to the freshly planted seeds and then to the large elm tree, "and strong."

"But how can I? Everyone here either doesn't trust me or, worse, hates me," Nog countered.

Boothby clipped a yellow flower from the bed and handed it to Nog. "All those things they mock you for are your greatest assets. Remember,

"THAT'S UNBELIEVABLE. WHO WOULD BE FOOLISH ENOUGH TO PICK A FIGHT WITH *WORF*?"

energy, each missing the others' target. Nog climbed on a high pedestal that reminded him of the Promenade on DS9. From that vantage point, he saw Ford walking tentatively along a cliff's edge below.

Nog called out, "Hey Ford, here's a note for you!" He pressed the trigger on his phaser, landing a direct hit on Ford. "I'm not going anywhere!"

The cave disintegrated into the yellow and black grid pattern of the holodeck as Commander Runnels' voice boomed over the holodeck comms system, "Congratulations, Cadet Nog! You are the sole survivor and have received the highest points in this exam."

Nog strode out of the simulation

room, into the waiting corridor. There, he saw most of the other cadets glaring at him. But, for the first time since he arrived on Earth, their looks of disdain didn't bother him, and there were even a couple, like Whitaker, who were actually *smiling*!

* * *

The following day, Nog found Boothby watering the seeds they'd planted together.

"Booth-by!" he called. "I have wonderful news!"

Boothby grunted an acknowledgement before Nog regaled him with the events of the test.

"You were right! Every part of

me is as valuable as latinum," Nog declared. "Even more valuable!"

Boothby nodded as Nog continued, "I know the other cadets won't accept me overnight, but they will eventually. It's what makes Starfleet, Starfleet!"

Nog noticed Boothby shifting his watering to a bed of the yellow flowers like the one the groundskeeper had given him a few days earlier.

"By the way, what are those flowers called?" he asked. "They bloom so quickly."

Boothby turned to face him, and said, simply, "Daylily Ferengi Gold."

"Ferengi Gold," Nog said with a grin. "I like that." ⊀

WORK WORTH DOING

STORY BY
KEITH
R.A. DECANDIDO

STORY: KEITH R.A. DECANDIDO
ILLUSTRATION: LOUIE DE MARTINIS

3190

Ambassador Laira Rillak sat in the reception area outside the office of Federation President Ligg, trying very hard not to fidget.

Ligg's assistant – like the president herself, a native of Tellar, the only founding member world still in the Federation – touched her ear and then said, "The president will see you now, Madam Ambassador."

Rillak smiled and nodded as she slowly got to her feet, walking past the assistant's desk to the doors that parted at her approach.

Inside, the elderly Tellarite woman who'd led the Federation for six terms was sitting at her desk reading a holo display. At Rillak's entrance, she stood and waved away first the holo, then her entire desk and chair, reprogramming the latter into two comfortable chairs. "Madam Ambassador, thank you for coming. Please have a seat."

"My pleasure, Madam President." Rillak sat in one of the seats. A replicator prompt appeared over one of the armrests, and she said, "Tarkalean tea, hot."

The beverage materialized on the armrest. As Rillak took a sip, Ligg said, "Raktajino, with a jacarine peel."

Setting her cup down, Rillak smiled. "I didn't know you liked Klingon coffee, Madam President."

"I like to vary my drink choices. But we're not here to talk about beverages. I want your honest opinion – what do you think of Governor Tira?"

The request for honesty notwithstanding, Rillak chose her words regarding the elected leader of Denobula Triaxa

carefully. "Denobula has remained very stable under his leadership – no mean feat in these times. That's probably why he's so popular."

"What of Councilor Hrak-Nat?"

Now wondering why she was being quizzed about random politicians, Rillak said of Brikar's representative on the Federation Council: "She's very blunt, but also very proactive. She's been at the forefront of every effort to expand the Federation, and that's been on overdrive since the Verubin Nebula." She took a sip of tea, then decided to just ask. "Madam President, why are you asking me about those two in particular?"

"Tomorrow, they will both be officially announced as candidates running for Federation President."

Somehow, Rillak managed not to scoff derisively. "Why would they even consider running against you?"

"Because I'm not running again."

3138

Fifteen-year-old Laira Rillak saw that the bay doors to *Hebitian Pride* weren't yet shut. Dad had put her in charge of this run from their home on Alshallah to Toros III while he and Mom took a much-needed vacation to Lake Sisko. She immediately transported down to the cargo bay to find out what was going on.

Dad's cargomaster, a Lurian named Flicc, had his head in his hands, while two of Dad's clients – a Ferengi woman, Brya, and Dad's cousin Mareq, a Cardassian – were arguing with each other. Like many members of Dad's extended family, Mareq followed the Bajoran religion, and wore an ornate earring on his left ear.

"What's going on?" Laira asked Flicc.

Before Flicc could say anything, Mareq said, "Oh thank the Prophets, you're here, Laira. Tell this Ferengi that I have priority."

"Priority for what? Both of you have cargo going to Toros."

Brya pointed an accusing finger at the Cardassian. "Two of his cargo containers are occupying the space for my tulaberry wine!"

Turning to Flicc, Laira asked, "Do you have the manifest?"

The Lurian activated a holo display and cast it to Laira.

Laira studied the display, then looked at both clients. "Uncle Mareq, you were only supposed to have six containers of stembolts. This says you have eight."

Mareq shrugged. "My client increased the order at the last minute. It happens sometimes. Your father always gives me the extra space."

Brya threw up her hands. "I knew it! I knew you'd pull the family card! I should've gone with a Ferengi

carrier – one who knows the Rules of Acquisition!"

Laira grinned. "Like the one about how you shouldn't let family get in the way of opportunity? The Sixth Rule, right?"

With respect, Brya said, "You know the Rules."

"Yes, and I know the Four Hundred and Nineteenth Rule, too: 'It's easier to get forgiveness than permission.'" She rotated the holo toward Brya. "You were only supposed to have ten cases of tulaberry wine, not fifteen."

"Ha!" Mareq sneered at the Ferengi. "So she lied! She doesn't deserve the space."

"Not so fast, Uncle Mareq, you lied, too."

"I didn't lie, I underestimated. Look, let's just call your father. I'm sure he'll settle this."

"*I'm* in charge of this run, Uncle

Mareq. Besides, it's the middle of the night on Lake Sisko, and I'm not waking him and Mom for this." *Mom will kill both of us*, she thought with a shudder. Her parents had been planning this vacation for over a year.

Brya said, "I'm willing to hold back three cases of wine."

"I'm not willing to hold back anything!" Mareq snapped. "My client *needs* these stembolts! I'm not going to let anything stand in the way of fulfilling this order."

Laira ran some projections. "Brya, it's fine. You can have all fifteen cases. We can make the room, as long as Uncle Mareq keeps to his assigned cargo space."

"But what about my other two containers?" Mareq asked.

"They'll go in your cabin."

Mareq's eyes went wide. "They won't fit!"

"Oh, they will, after we lose the

"I LIKE TO VARY MY DRINK CHOICES. BUT WE'RE NOT HERE TO TALK ABOUT BEVERAGES. I WANT YOUR HONEST OPINION..."

bunk and desk and commode. They'll fit perfectly, in fact." She showed Mareq the specs she'd just worked out.

"Where am I supposed to bunk?"

"We can set up a hammock somewhere, and you can use the crew commode."

"That is not acceptable!"

Laira tilted her head. "You *just said* that you wouldn't let anything stand in the way of fulfilling this order. That would include your comfort, right?"

"I – " Mareq stared angrily at her. "Your father's going to hear about this."

As the Cardassian stormed off, Laira looked at Flicc. "Have two of Mareq's containers transported to his cabin."

Flicc nodded.

"Computer, reset the programmable matter in guest cabin four to empty."

"Acknowledged."

Brya bowed her head to Laira. "Thank you, Ms. Rillak. I guess you understand the Sixth Rule after all."

"I also know that you're bringing *twenty* cases, and the other five are in *your* cabin. That's where I got the idea."

With that, Laira transported out of the cargo bay. She needed to get this run going…

3190

"What do you mean you're not running?"

President Ligg chuckled. "I'm a hundred and forty-seven years old, Laira. I'm *tired*."

"But – the Burn is over! The Federation's finally expanding for the first time in a century! This is what you've been *waiting* for!"

"It's what I've been *hoping* for. But that hope was buried *so* deep." She shook her head. "The thought of leading the Federation through what comes next, frankly, exhausts me. And if just thinking about it does that, then actually doing it will probably kill me." She chuckled again. "No, we need fresh blood. We need *you*, Laira."

Rillak blinked. "Excuse me? You just said that Tira and Hrak were running. For that matter, there's Vice President Qiladar."

"Qiladar's retiring also. As for the others, Tira is too passive. He's popular, yes, but his strength comes from staying the course, which is what's been needed. But we can't afford someone who will remain so status quo now. As for Hrak-Nat, she's too far in the other direction. She bullies her way into getting what she needs for her constituents on Brikar, and doesn't care who gets in

the way. That works for a member of the Federation Council, but not for the council's leader. With Ni'Var and Trill on the cusp of rejoining, talks with United Earth progressing, and with the Emerald Chain broken, we need someone who will bring sides together." She put a hand on Rillak's shoulder. "We need the person who negotiated the border dispute between the Tholians and the Betazoids."

3169

The holographic image of the Tholian made a screeching noise that Rillak felt in her ribs. "Who are you?"

"I'm Coun – I mean, Federation Ambassador Laira Rillak." Vice President Qiladar had only sworn Rillak in to her new post as Federation Ambassador-at-Large a day ago. "I'm replacing Ambassador Chynskai."

The other holo in the room was the Prime Minister of Betazed, Lwarafarakna Vill, who bowed her head. *"I was sorry to learn of Chynskai's death. She was a good woman."*

The Tholian – whom the briefing material said was named Sraklene – made another screeching noise. "She was rigid. You will not be, lest we walk away from these talks."

"I have no wish to be rigid. Let us begin by completing the introductions,"

Tholians. It has made negotiations impossible."

"The contempt," the Tholian said, "was Srakelene's. I am Captain Zrelarn. Let us speak and let us solve."

Rillak smiled. "Yes. Let's."

3190

"Final question for the three candidates." The moderator read off the holoprompter. "How would you convince worlds that have left the Federation, such as Ni'Var and Andor, to rejoin? Governor Tira?"

None of the three presidential candidates were in the chamber with the moderator. Tira was in his home on Denobula Triaxa IX; Hrak-Nat was on her personal yacht somewhere in the Brikar system; Rillak was in her living room on Alshallah. All were being projected into the chamber, and this debate was being projected into locations both private and public all over the thirty-eight worlds of the Federation, as well as some places outside it.

With a disturbingly wide smile, the Denobulan said, "Oh, I think the benefits to joining the Federation speak for themselves – especially now that dilithium is becoming readily available once again."

"Councilor Hrak-Nat?"

The woman with the rock-hard skin rose from her giant chair and spoke in what almost sounded like a growl. "It's been a hundred years, I don't think anything the Federation does can be said to speak for itself. We must push back out into the stars, and we should start by annexing what's left of the Emerald Chain. That, along with the dilithium mining in the Verubin Nebula, will give us the resources to properly rebuild. We can finally go back to doing what we did best in the old days: bring people in."

"Ambassador Rillak?"

Rillak waited for Hrak to sit back down. "We can't expect people to come to us, and we can't force them, either. The Federation is an idea, an important one, and it's one that's been lost since the Burn. Councilor Hrak-Nat is correct that we cannot simply sit by and wait for worlds to come to us – but we can't go out

said Rillak. "I already know Minister Vill, but I'm afraid your government didn't update us as to who Sraklene's replacement would be."

The Tholian was silent.

Rillak continued. "Your dorsal chitin reflects differently than Sraklene's. If I recall correctly, that means that you're a military captain, rather than a diplomat, like Sraklene. I hope this doesn't mean that the Tholian Assembly is going to take a more hardline approach to this border dispute with Betazed. I also must admit to finding it puzzling that you switched negotiators without alerting us. Did you think we wouldn't notice?"

The Tholian remained silent.

Then the holo flickered and disappeared.

Rillak felt panic suffuse her entire person. She was *extremely* grateful that Vill was on Betazed rather than in the room with her, as it wouldn't do for the minister to telepathically sense her fear that she had blown her first diplomatic assignment.

She hadn't even wanted to become a representative on Alshallah

a decade ago, but when Dad retired, it seemed the thing to do.

And now she was an ambassador, and she had apparently wasted no time in pissing off the Tholians.

Only a few seconds passed, though it felt like hours, and the Tholian reappeared. "I did warn Sraklene. He said you could not tell us apart. I have told him he was wrong."

Vill said, "This is what we have had to deal with, Madam Ambassador: the contempt the Tholians have for all who are *not*

> "MY CLIENT NEEDS THESE STEMBOLTS! I'M NOT GOING TO LET ANYTHING STAND IN THE WAY OF FULFILLING THIS ORDER."

and force them, either. For far too long, the Federation has – by necessity – been isolationist. But that will make it difficult for people to trust us. We haven't *been* the Federation, not really. We've had to compromise, to sacrifice. And we'll have to do that some more, but now we can do it from a place of compassion instead of fear. We can offer freedom, and we can offer dilithium – and for many, the latter will be more appealing than the former. However, it would be a mistake to try to force anyone's hand. We should reach out, absolutely, but that's the starting point. We should speak, and then we can solve."

3191

President-Elect Rillak stood behind the stage in Federation Headquarters, next to the Tellarite woman she'd be replacing.

President Ligg looked at her with concern and compassion behind her sunken eyes. "Are you ready, Laira?"

Rillak took a deep breath. "I – I'm not. Madam President, I don't – I don't

want this job."

Grinning, Ligg said, "Leaving that a bit late, aren't you? You won the election. Quite handily, I might add. And you can handle the responsibility."

"I don't mind responsibility. It's the power that scares me."

"Trust me, the position isn't *that* powerful," Ligg said with a snort. "Are you worried that it will corrupt?"

"No, that it'll overwhelm." Rillak sighed. "There's so much at stake. I'm not sure I'm the right person to lead this – this rebuild."

"Of course you are. Your entire career has been about finding ways to turn disagreements into agreements. *That's* what the Federation needs right now." Ligg leaned in and spoke in a conspiratorial whisper. "And we need your doubts, too. One reason why I was worried about Tira or Hrak taking my place is that they're both too sure of themselves – Tira to stay the course, Hrak to barrel ahead. But you? You're the right person for the job

precisely because you *don't* think you're the right person for the job."

On the stage, the vice president had finished being sworn in. It was now Rillak's turn.

She followed Ligg onto the stage. The entire Federation Council – including Hrak-Nat, who had given an uncharacteristically gracious concession speech – was present, as were representatives from all over the sector. Even President T'Rina of Ni'Var and Leader Pav of Trill – both still in talks to rejoin the Federation – were here to see her take the oath of office.

As she approached the podium, she found herself reminded of words spoken by a leader on her mother's ancestral home of Earth thirteen hundred years earlier: "Far and away the best prize that life has to offer is the chance to work hard at work worth doing."

This, she thought, *is work worth doing. Time I started doing it – whether I'm ready or not.* ⭑

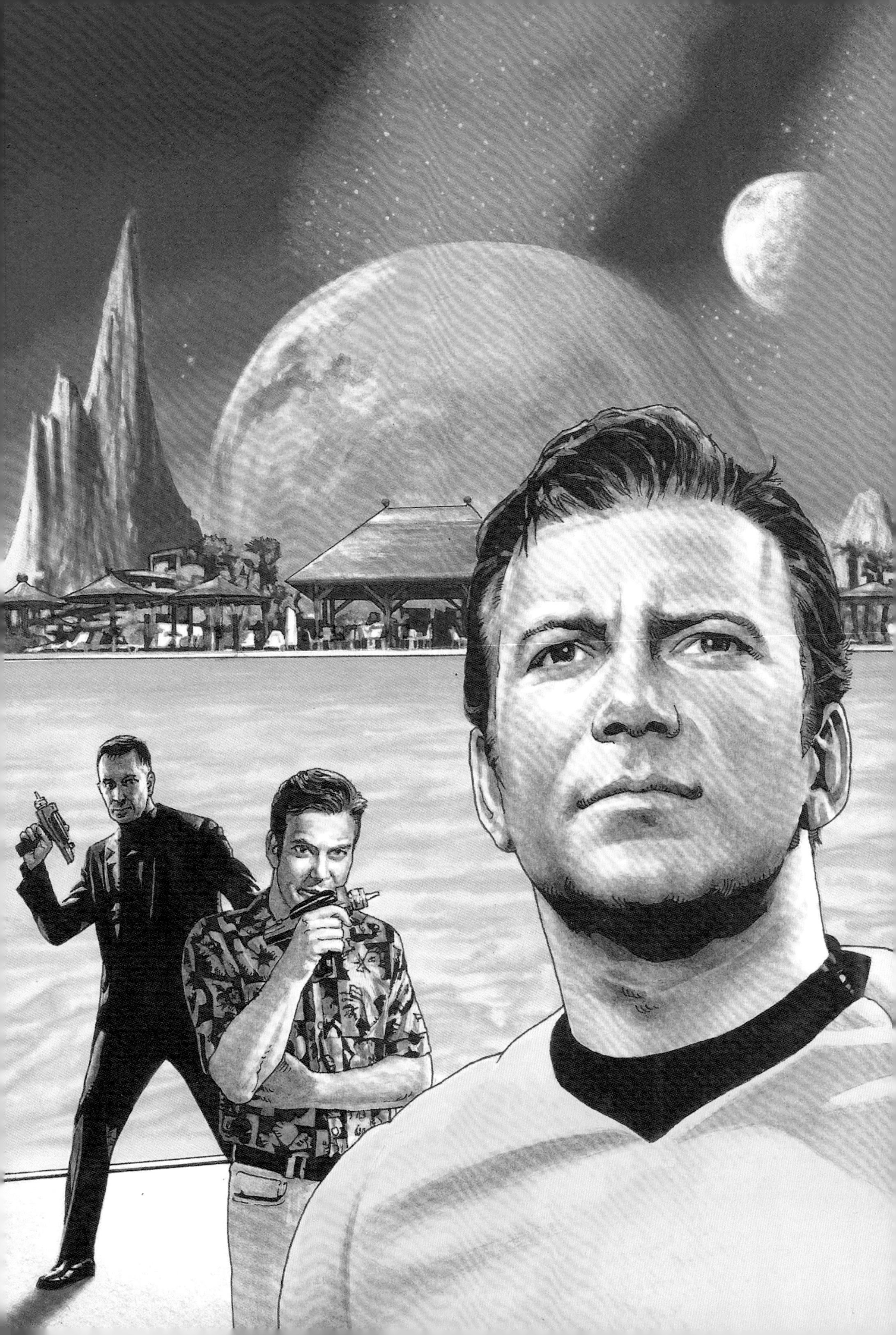

The Trouble with Jones

STORY: GREG COX
ILLUSTRATION: ANDY WALKER

aptain Kirk! Friend Kirk!"

Kirk groaned. He'd been enjoying shore leave at a tropical beach resort on Siduri, an independent world only loosely affiliated with the Federation, until he recognized an all-too-familiar voice.

Cyrano Jones, interstellar trader and general nuisance, beamed at Kirk from a beachside shack roofed with crimson palm fronds. The portly merchant seemed genuinely pleased to see Kirk, which was rather puzzling considering their history.

"Jones." The captain approached the shack warily. Hand-lettered driftwood signs advertised fruity drinks, clams, and trinkets – at suspiciously reasonable prices. Kirk was pleasantly surprised to see no tribbles in evidence. "What are you doing here?"

"Enjoying the good life, captain!" Jones stepped out from behind the counter in front of the shack. Given the balmy climate, he had swapped his usual olive coat for a gaudy floral-patterned shirt, knee-length shorts, and sandals. He gestured grandly at sand, sea, sun, and sky. "Who could ask for anything more?"

A pint-sized Andorian girl, no more than seven years old, interrupted the reunion, tugging on his arm.

"Excuse me, Mister Cyrano?" She held up a small wooden carving of an Aquan mer-princess, crowned with polished seashell fragments. "How much is she?"

"A mere two credits, little darling," Jones said. "And a bargain at that."

Her antennae drooped. "Oh. I only have half a credit. I spent the rest of my allowance on kelp frosties."

The girl's forlorn expression had Kirk reaching for his own local currency, but Jones spoke up first. "Hold on. Did I neglect to mention my shiny-smile discount, available only to the best little girls? A big grin knocks the price down to... exactly one-quarter credit!"

Bemused, Kirk looked on as the delighted child wandered off, clutching her prize.

"That was... unexpectedly... generous of you, Jones." The Cyrano Jones he knew was always out to make a fast credit, even if it meant playing fast and loose with the law and public safety. Granted, Jones had once provided Uhura with a complimentary tribble, but only with an eye to drumming up sales. Kirk couldn't see any long-term advantage to essentially giving the carved mermaid away. "Business doing that well?"

He found it hard to believe that the unprepossessing snack shack could be all that lucrative. Jones wasn't going to get rich off it.

Jones shrugged. "I make a modest living. Clam-digging, beachcombing, and the like. But what more do I truly need? Credits aren't everything after all."

Kirk was still trying to process that when a middle-aged couple in beach attire strolled by. They waved cheerily at Jones.

"Hi, Cyrano!" the man called out. "Thanks again for helping out at the reefs the other day! We really appreciate it!"

"Always a pleasure to assist my friends and neighbors!" he replied.

"You coming to the glow-tide feast tomorrow night?" the woman asked.

"Wouldn't miss it for a dozen worlds! Can't wait to partake of your famous anemone punch!"

Kirk felt as though he'd accidentally beamed into yet another mirror universe. Cyrano Jones, an asset to his community, getting by as a genial beach bum, not conniving to make a killing?

He didn't buy it. "What are you up to, Jones?"

"What can I say, captain? I'm a changed man, who regrets whatever difficulties I may have caused you in the past."

As a rule, Jones' exaggerated bonhomie had always been transparently self-serving, but this time Kirk heard nothing but sincerity in his voice.

"Are you . . . feeling well, Jones?"

"Never better! And healthy as a Horta!"

Kirk debated how to proceed. As far as he knew, Jones still had outstanding warrants for his arrest, dating back to his unauthorized exit from Deep Space Station K7, but Siduri was not under the Federation's jurisdiction and extraditing Jones might be more trouble than it was worth. Plus, Kirk was on vacation, out of uniform, and unarmed. He had his communicator in case the *U.S.S. Enterprise* needed to contact

him in an emergency or vice versa, but was a "reformed" Cyrano Jones an emergency?

"Jones, you double-crossing slime devil! Did you really think you could get away from me?"

A furious stranger stormed toward Jones, clearly with a score to settle.

"Friend Hastings!" Jones said somewhat sheepishly. "What brings you to Siduri?"

"Don't give me that 'friend'

hogwash! Friends don't ditch their business partners on a backwater planet in the middle of nowhere – and make off with the product!"

Now that sounds like Jones, Kirk thought.

Hastings was a nondescript fellow whose rumpled brown suit looked out of place on the beach. Kirk thought he looked vaguely familiar, but couldn't immediately place the name or face. He lingered to see how this awkward encounter

played out.

"Not my finest moment," Jones conceded, "but can't we let bygones be bygones? Allow me to offer you a cooling libation, on the house."

"I don't want a drink. I want what you stole from me." Hastings drew a phaser beneath his suit. "Where is it?"

"Hold on!" Kirk intervened. "Let's not lose our heads here. Put the phaser away before matters get too out of hand."

"Mind your own business, mister!" Hastings glared at Kirk, after ignoring him before. His eyes widened in recognition. Hatred contorted his face.

"Kirk! You ruined my life, you arrogant bastard!"

> "WHAT CAN I SAY, CAPTAIN? I'M A CHANGED MAN, WHO REGRETS WHATEVER DIFFICULTIES I MAY HAVE CAUSED YOU IN THE PAST."

A phaser beam knocked the captain out cold.

* * *

"I'm telling you for the last time, Jones! Give me back what's mine!"

Kirk awoke to find both he and Jones taped to surprisingly sturdy posts in the back of Jones's shack. His communicator rested atop a kitchen counter, out of reach.

"I would be delighted to oblige, but, regretfully, that is not so easily accomplished…"

"No excuses, Jones! I want those spores!"

Spores?

Kirk belatedly remembered where he knew Hastings from. The man was one of the colonists relocated from Omicron Ceti III a few years ago, after being liberated from the tranquilizing influence of the mind-altering spores found on that world.

Could those same spores be responsible for Jones' easy-going new attitude?

"The Omicron Ceti spores?" Kirk interrupted. "My understanding was that those couldn't grow or thrive outside their native environment, which had been inundated by Berthold rays?"

"I was working on that!" Hastings insisted. "Given sufficient time and resources, I can find a way to grow them elsewhere, beyond the meddling reach of the Federation. Or that was the plan before Jones betrayed me."

Jones offered a nervous smile. "I wouldn't quite put it that way."

"How else would you describe it?" Hastings appeared eager to vent. "Do you know how hard it was to smuggle a pod plant off the planet

"DON'T GIVE ME THAT 'FRIEND' HOGWASH! FRIENDS DON'T DITCH THEIR BUSINESS PARTNERS ON A BACKWATER PLANET IN THE MIDDLE OF NOWHERE – AND MAKE OFF WITH THE PRODUCT!"

during the evacuation, right under the nose of Kirk's Starfleet goons? Then I had the bad luck to run into you. *You* convinced me that the spores had commercial potential, with their gift of tranquility and perfect health, right before absconding with the pod and leaving me in the lurch!" He waved the phaser in Jones' face. "So where are my spores?"

"Well, if you must know, the spacecraft I 'borrowed' to seek out new investors ran into a spot of interstellar turbulence and the pod's container spilled open during the flight…"

"And you got exposed to your own product," Kirk deduced.

"And the pod?" Hastings asked anxiously. "What happened to it?"

"The poor thing expired, I'm afraid. I did my best to nurture it, but, as you recall, it was already ailing when I… took it off your hands as it were. So you see there's nothing left to quarrel over. Easy come, easy go."

"Probably just as well." Kirk attempted to reason with Hastings. "Omicron Ceti III was evacuated with good reason. Those spores had sapped you of all drive and ambition, the very

traits that led you to seek a new life on a new world in the first place."

Hasting wheeled about to confront Kirk. "Who were you to judge, Kirk? I was happy there, happier than I'd ever been. You robbed me of paradise!"

Hastings turned the phaser on Kirk. He switched the setting from Stun to Kill.

"Funny thing, Kirk, I wouldn't want revenge if I was still on spores. Too bad for –"

There was a knock at the door.

"Hello, Cyrano?" The voice belonged to one of the friendly neighbors who had strolled by earlier. "Sorry to drop in unannounced, but we brought you a fresh pot of my anemone broth, since you were so looking forward to it."

Hastings gave his captives a warning look, holding a finger to his lips.

"Cyrano? Are you all right? Why aren't you coming to the door?"

Hastings swore under his breath. "Don't breathe a word, either of you, while I get rid of these pests. Unless you want them to share your fate."

He headed out front, leaving Kirk and Jones alone in the back.

"This is our chance." Kirk tested his bonds, which proved far too secure. "We need to think fast, before he gets back."

"But what can we do?" Jones threw up his hands, figuratively. "It seems our time has come, captain. Whatever will be, will be."

"Blast it! I don't need a kinder, gentler Cyrano Jones right now. I need the crafty survivor who always lands on his feet."

And Kirk knew there was only way to get that Cyrano back.

"I should have realized you'd be useless in a pinch, Jones. You're a disgrace: an oily, small-time grifter who's been nothing but trouble since the day we met!"

"Friend Kirk!"

Jones' pained expression made Kirk feel like he was kicking a puppy, but he persisted – for both their sakes.

"You call yourself a changed man? Don't make me laugh. You're still the same pathetic embarrassment you've always been, just weaker and more helpless!"

"Really, Captain, there's no call for that kind of language."

"I'm just getting started. You have less spine than a tribble and fewer scruples than a Klingon. You're a worthless, no-account, double-dealing –"

"Now see here, Kirk!" Jones flushed with anger. "I won't stand for –" He paused and blinked in confusion, as good, old-fashioned fury burned away his bliss, just as it had with Spock years ago. The color drained from Jones' face. "What in perdition have I been doing?"

"Welcome back, Jones," Kirk said.

And none too soon. Kirk overheard snatches of conversation as Hastings sent Jones' unsuspecting visitors on their way. "Cyrano's all tied up at present, but I'll make sure he gets that broth. Me? Oh, I'm an old friend of his."

A few pleasantries later, he was back with his phaser. "Now then, where were we?"

"You were about to throw away the opportunity of a lifetime, my short-sighted friend," Jones said. "Kirk is too valuable to be disintegrated out of mere spite. The Romulans, the Klingons, the Orions… there's no shortage of parties who will pay a fortune for the classified Starfleet secrets in

Kirk's head, assuming, that is, you have the connections and expertise to properly auction him off to the highest bidder." He puffed out his chest. "Which, as it happens, I have in abundance."

"Seriously? You're asking me to trust you again?"

"What's past is past. You need to think about the future, Friend Hastings, and the positively galactic profits in the offing."

Hastings appeared intrigued despite himself. "Even if I was willing to consider this, who is going to finance this endeavor? I spent my last credit tracking you to Siduri."

"There's a strongbox hidden at the back of the pantry, holding

valuables in anticipation of a hasty departure. Spican flame gems, Elasian aphrodisiacs, and such. See for yourself if you don't believe me."

"You bet I will."

Jones directed him to the strongbox. "The pass code is 'glommer,' by the way."

Greed got the better of Hastings. Placing the box on a table, he keyed in the combination, only to get a face full of swirling orange vapor. Gasping, he staggered backwards.

A boobytrap, Kirk surmised. He held his breath as the gas swiftly dispersed.

Hasting's face went slack, his eyes glassy.

"A mild hypnotic," Jones explained, "rendering him briefly susceptible to suggestion."

"Suggestion," Hastings echoed robotically.

Jones demonstrated the gas's effect by having Hastings free him from the post, then hand over his phaser, which Jones promptly employed to stun him. "Pleasant dreams."

Kirk remained bound, however, and at Jones's mercy. To his surprise, however, Jones loosened Kirk's bonds somewhat. "There now. You should be able to extricate yourself . . . eventually. In the meantime, I'll help myself to your communicator, to

allow me a decent head start before you can contact the *Enterprise.*"

"I don't understand," Kirk said. "You don't want to get back at me for our past run-ins, not to mention everything I just called you? What happened to auctioning me off to the highest bidder?"

"Moi?" Jones clutched his heart, as though shocked by the very notion. "Besides, I owe you one, Kirk, for breaking those spores' abominable spell over me. You saw what they turned me into: a guileless layabout, more interested in sunsets than credits."

A shudder ran through him. "It was *ghastly!*" ★

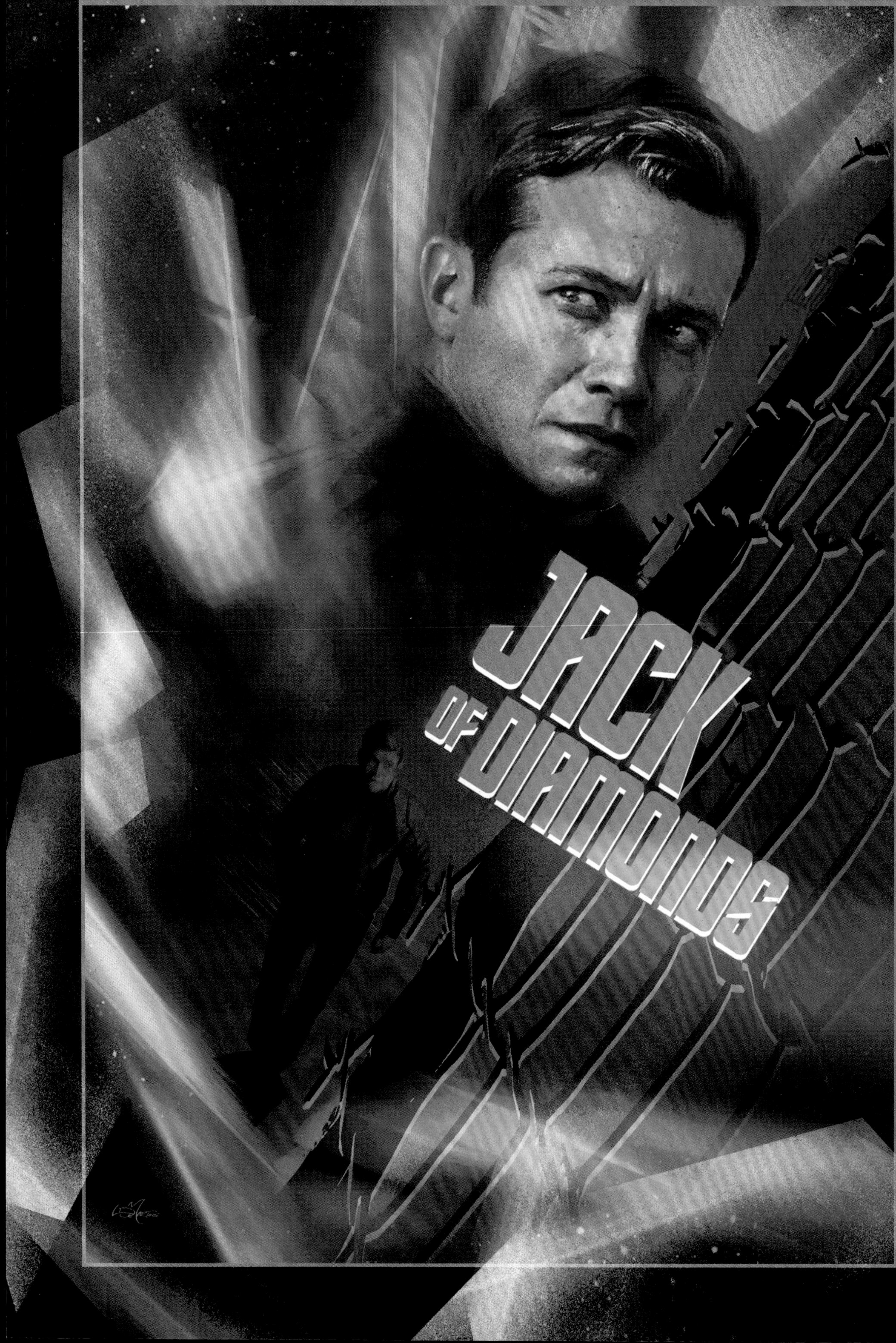
JACK
OF DIAMONDS

Jack of Diamonds

WORDS: UNA MCCORMACK
ART: LOUIE DE MARTINIS

(SET JUST PRIOR TO THE EVENTS OF STAR TREK: PICARD, 'THE NEXT GENERATION'.)

ack Crusher, looking at the high fence rising up in front of him, was starting to entertain the possibility that there was the slightest of chances that very soon he might be in a spot of bother.

"What's happening, Jack?"

Jack was nimble, Jack was quick – but tonight Jack was slowed down by the heavy bag on his back and Jack would be damned before he surrendered his treasures. He had put a lot of effort into laying his hands on them and if their previous owners wanted them back, they could prize them out of his cold… Well. Best not go there. Best not push his luck too far.

Jack considered the fence. On a good day, he could scale a fence like this with the agility of a long-legged Hylarian tree-frog. Tonight, however, he had to haul himself up like a lump of Tratian lead. In general, Jack preferred his getaways to be stylish, but since the point of a getaway was to… well, *get away*, he was going to have to be content with something considerably cruder. He paused, one leg either side of the fence, to catch his breath. Greasy, smog-filled air. This place was a dump. Why were these places always such dumps? Where was his Risian holiday?

"Jack! Talk to me!"

"Give us a moment," Jack muttered. He peered back through the gloom and the grubby orange lamplight. Had he lost them? No such luck. There they were – covering the ground between the bar that Jack had lately visited and the spot where he was currently perched, and moving like a pair of gazelles…

Scratch that. Jack was the gazelle. Those chaps were the bloody *cheetahs*…

"Why," mumbled Jack, pulling himself over the fence and dropping heavily to the ground on the other side, "are these people always so damn well *fit*?"

"Jack! What's going on?"

Fit, and *quick*…

"Fine," Jack lied, looking round – for a place to go or a place to hide. "Everything's fine. Just… taking stock of the universe and my place in it."

"You know, that didn't answer my question."

Right. So. Nowhere to hide. Not here. Next option (actually, only other option) – run.

Jack ran.

"I was hoping… you wouldn't… notice that…"

"I'm your mother. I notice everything. Like the fact that you're now running."

She did notice everything, that was true. She was like an owl, his mother, head moved round slowly, but covered one hundred and eighty degrees, and invariably caught him in the middle of some mischief or other… Not to mention annoyingly wise. Still, there were some things she had never seen (God, Jack hoped so), and some things he preferred not to mention. Like the fact that this little mission was – truth be told – swerving in the direction of becoming a bit of a disaster and Jack wasn't yet sure if/how he was going to get himself out of this one…

"Who are you running from this time, Jack?"

"Just… trying to stay… *fit*…"

But he *would* get himself out of trouble. Definitely. Jack *always* got himself out of trouble.

"Do you need anything from me?"

More or less.

Jack, choosing his direction and running full pelt, thought, *You could stop yapping for a minute…*

"Jack, you were meant to be back on board Eleos *by now. We can't stay in one place for too long. We can't hang around."*

Jack wasn't hanging around; Jack was running like the clappers, down this alleyway, while behind him came the yells of his erstwhile friends and drinking partners. *This way! Come on! We can get him!"*

Jack kept on running for as long as he could. Until:

"Ah."

"Jack? Is something wrong?"

"Oh, no, nothing's wrong," said Jack, cheerfully. "By which I mean I'm in what you might, er, call… a bit of dead-end situation."

"What?"

"I've run into a dead end. You know. You run up an alley and then the alley, well… *stops?"*

Pause there. Mother taking stock. He pictured her head, moving round slowly, one-eighty degrees. She'd get there…

"Why is that a problem, Jack? You said you had the package and that you were coming straight back."

Now, there was nothing wrong, *per se*, with finding yourself at one end of an alley facing a brick wall. The problem only arose under certain circumstances. Like – to pluck an example out of the thin dark industrial air – if you'd recently gone for a drink and met some chaps and played a couple of rounds of cards and won something useful from them and then they'd kind of maybe worked out that your patter and your chatter were a cover for something possibly leaning towards the dodgy about the cards that you were playing with, and the thing about that was people got antsy and very quickly you found yourself being chased through the greasy orange night of a yet another dumpsville planet… Then (and, again, Jack was offering this purely as an example), *then* you might find that being at one end of an alley facing a brick wall was what you might call a problem.

"Jack!"

Also, his mother was on his case. As ever.

Oh, dear, though. Here they were. Two big fellows, and they didn't look half as friendly as they had but an hour ago, when Jack was paying for the drinks… Everything was fine, though. Everything was going to be fine. Because Jack had discovered, over the years, that tricky situations came in two types. The first were the ones you could run away from…

"Jack Crusher," said perhaps the least of his problems, *"you tell me right now what's going on, or I swear to God I'll—"*

"Mum," said Jack.

"Oh dear," sighed his mother. Jack only ever used 'mum' as a prelude to bad news.

"Yeah."

"Go on."

"Mum, remember that time I got caught cheating at cards?"

Pause again. Like she was working her way through *multiple times*, or something…

"Which time exactly are we talking about?"

Oh, mother dearest, you really are *quite* hilarious… "I mean, the first time."

This pause was a lot less fun. The first time Jack got caught at cards was after –

"Yes," said his mother quietly. *"I remember."*

"Now that was a right old situation, wasn't it?"

"As I recall, yes." His mother sighed. *"Jack –"*

Those chaps were close now.

"I'm thinking that this situation might very soon be analogous." But that was all right too. That was also perfectly fine. Because the *second* type of tricky situation –

"You told me you'd done a deal," said his mother.

"It wasn't a lie," he said. "Not exactly."

"Cheating at cards isn't the same as doing a deal!"

"That depends on how you look at it."

"How do you think the people on the other end of your goddamn sleight of hand look at it?"

"I'm sure they can be persuaded

> "I'M YOUR MOTHER. I NOTICE *EVERYTHING*. LIKE THE FACT THAT YOU'RE NOW RUNNING."

to see the funny side."

She sighed, deeply. *"Jack…"* she said, almost in despair.

I am what you made me, mother dearest… Aren't you proud?

Jack looked at the two men heading his way and smiled. Because the second type of tricky situation and (this was definitely, no question, the second type) was the one you talked yourself out of. And Jack loved the sound of his own voice. His voice was basically his *superpower…*

"All right," said his mother, *"I'm beaming you back on board* Eleos *right now."*

"What?" Jack frowned. "Don't do that!"

"This has gone far enough –

"I'll be fine!"

"You're going to get hurt!"

Big chaps, though, these two; you had to admit that. Carrying – what did you call those things? Koshes? Cudgels? Not nice, whatever they were. Yes, Jack thought – he might get hurt. But she had to come to terms with that, didn't she, mummy dearest? She must have known it came with the territory. That if you saddled yourself with a kid (and, by the way, it wasn't like he was her *first*), you realized that eventually they were going to get hurt.

"If you beam me up now, *mother*, you'll reveal your location. Whoever's after us – they'll know where *Eleos* is. And you might recall that we've gone to some trouble to *prevent* that."

This was what happened, if (for whatever mad reason) you decided to keep the kid. You had to accept that at some point they were going to get hurt and there wasn't anything you could do about that, what with people being finite and so on…

"I don't care if they find out where Eleos is –"

Apart from her other son. He wasn't finite, was he? But Jack was…

"Well, I bloody well *do*! Listen – I got myself into this. I'll get myself out."

"What are you going to do, huh? Negotiate with them?"

"Why not?" he said, and thought: *Isn't that would daddy dearest*

would do? "Gift of the gab, me."

The two men were now right front of him. Jack gave a crooked smile. Oh yes. He could *definitely* talk his way out of this…

"Gentlemen," he said, palms opening in comradeship. "Surely we can sort this out amicably?"

One of those pauses. Those ineffable pauses, where everything hung in the balance, and Jack was completely sure that the universe would turn his way, that his winning hand would come up…

And then…

You haven't lived, thought Jack, *until you've seen a seven-fingered fist heading your way…*

Never landed though. Jack's winning hand came up – or, at least, the transporter beam caught him before that fist could.

Jack be nimble… Jack be quick…

"I told you," Jack snapped, "*not* to beam me back on board! They'll locate us –"

"Jack Crusher," said his mother, "if you think I've never reconfigured a transporter signal to give temporary cover, then you really don't have a good idea of who and what I am."

Yeah, thought Jack, *fine, all right – but do you always have to be so competent? So bloody wise?*

"You know, Jack," said Beverly Crusher, "one day I won't be there to save you."

"I know."

She drew him to her. The briefest of hugs. And whispered, into his hair, "I do remember, you know."

"Remember what?"

"The first time you got caught cheating at cards. After…"

Jack pulled away. It was after she'd told him who his father was. A teenager, and by the time she'd filled him in on the details, he was livid. Bit of a temper on him, at that age. Jack had worked hard on that. Didn't help, in the long run.

"Talked my way out of that one, didn't I?"

His mother looked at him, eyes wide in disbelief. "Is *that* what you remember happened?"

"Well, yes –" That's what always happened.

"Jack," she said. "I had to come and bail you out."

Jack frowned. "Are you sure?"

"Oh, I'm sure!"

"Ah. Okay. Well, thanks for the, er… thanks for the transporter reconfigurationment, or whatever it was that you did."

"You're welcome." She nodded at the bag on his back. "Is that what slowed you down?"

He swung it off his shoulder and placed it on the floor. "Thirty Cardassian disruptors. They'll come in handy, should we ever be in need of –"

A bribe.

"Currency," said his mother, firmly, and he let her have that lie. Why not? Her voice lowered, to whisper a secret nobody else must hear. "And what about the Dibarian crystals?"

He reached into his jacket to take out the little case, opening it like a magician pulling his best trick. There they lay, nestled inside, and sparkling, innocently. God, but they were beautiful. You'd take a fist in the face for these. Or not, as it happened. He smiled at his mother, and she smiled back.

"You asked. And I delivered."

Always have, mother dearest. And always will. ★

A Dish Served Cold

STORY: CHRIS DOWS

ILLUSTRATION: PETE WALLBANK

"Captain… a photon torpedo has armed in the storage racks!"

Kirk swiveled in his chair on the bridge of the *U.S.S. Enterprise*, and turned to Chekov, who looked toward him in disbelief. A beat, then Kirk stepped down and headed for the navigator's station as he barked an order.

"Disarm it, mister!"

Chekov hit a sequence of buttons.

"Override commands are not working, sir."

Repeating the pattern, Kirk got the same result and could feel the tension rising on the bridge. *Another* incident.

"Uhura, contact the torpedo bay. I want to know what's going on down there."

Within seconds, the communications officer turned from her controls, fingers pressed to her ear communicator.

"No response from the station, sir. The ordnance crew has received the alert and are on their way."

Kirk nodded; the torpedo room wasn't routinely manned, save for regular inspections.

"Get them to report the second they arrive."

As Uhura swiveled back to her console, Spock straightened from the scanner at his science station and stepped down towards the helm.

"If the proximity fuse has been set, any attempt to manually defuse the torpedo will detonate the device and cause a catastrophic chain reaction with the other ordnance. I would advise against this procedure, Captain."

Kirk considered Spock's caution. Trying to disarm the torpedo would only hasten the destruction of the ship.

"Uhura… belay that order. Tell the ordnance crew to stand by."

"Aye sir."

Sulu turned to Kirk, his voice clear and calm.

"Sir, could we load and launch it? The safety protocols should protect – "

"Helm, the protocols are clearly not operating within normal parameters. The outcome would likely be the same."

Kirk knew his first officer was, of course, correct, but Sulu's idea suggested another course of action.

"Spock… there's an external loading hatch for the torpedo racks. What if we opened it?"

Spock raised an eyebrow and considered Kirk's solution.

"The sudden decompressive pressure may trigger the weapon. It may also impact other inert torpedoes on its exit. However, the risks are no greater than a manual attempt at neutralizing it."

Kirk looked around the bridge. He had to decide – now.

"Uhura – issue an evacuation order to the saucer section. As soon as we're clear, blow the airlock Chekov."

The navigator's reply held no relief at the solution; everyone present knew this was trading one dangerous chance for another.

"Aye, sir."

* * *

Kirk strode into the briefing room, mood dark and jaw set firm. Glancing over to the alarm panel on the wall, he battled with the fear it might go off again at any time. Seated before him along the polished wooden table were Spock, Doctor McCoy and Mister Scott, his preoccupied chief engineer, who was studying a schematic on the three-way table monitor and tracing a circuit route with a dirty finger on the screen. As Kirk took his seat, Spock provided a situation update.

"The torpedo bay has been sealed, and damage to the forward shields is under repair. Efforts to trace the cause of the incident continue."

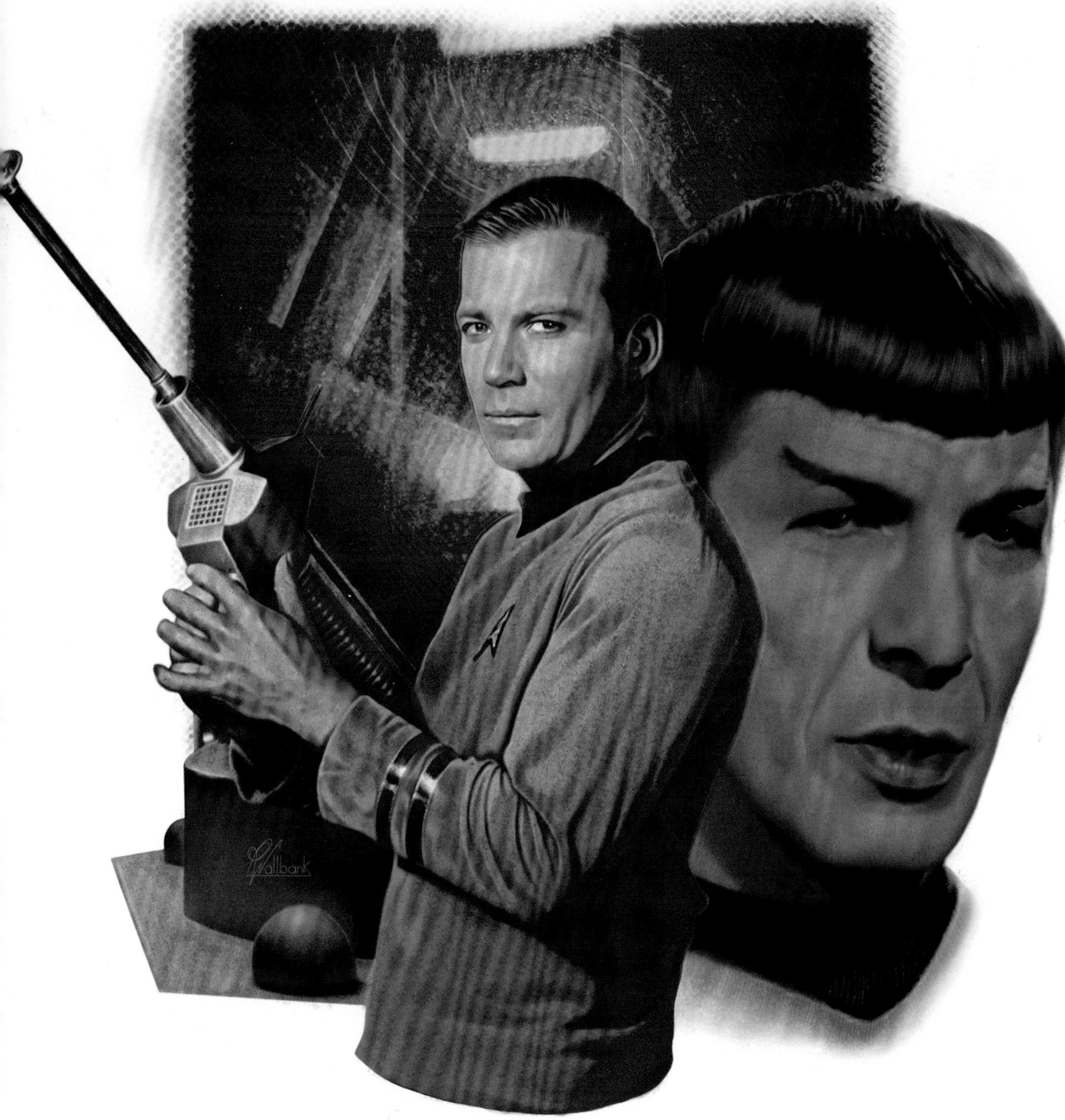
Wallbank

Kirk turned to Mr Scott, who sat back from the monitor and sighed.

"Anything further to report, Mister Scott?"

"No sir. Everything is pointing to the same conclusion, and I dinna like it one bit."

Kirk felt anger rise in his chest – not from the redoubtable engineer's comments, but the inevitability of the meeting's conclusion. Spock's reply did little to lighten the mood.

"An emotional response will not alter the facts, Engineer. No evidence of malfunction is presenting itself because it does not exist. Occam's razor, Mister Scott."

Mr Scott frowned, while McCoy nodded.

"Pains me to agree with you Spock, but you're right. The simplest explanation is usually the correct one. What are the chances of catastrophic failures in the deflector control, dilithium chamber safeties and photon torpedo bay all within seventy-two hours Mr Scott? From my understanding, these systems aren't even linked."

"Aye, you're right. Not directly, anyway. Just doesn't make sense."

Spock spread his slender fingers and joined them at their tips, lost in his thoughts. Mr Scott shifted uncomfortably in his chair and McCoy folded his arms. Kirk knew the level of anxiety throughout the ship might lead to yet more problems. It was time to take control of the situation, even if it meant stating an unwelcome truth.

"It's settled then. We have a saboteur on board my ship."

Scott's face darkened at the thought of such betrayal.

"Aye, but who? They'd need to know the *Enterprise* pretty well to do what they've done and not leave any tracks. I've reviewed all the duty logs and everyone in engineering is accounted for when the events occurred."

"Attacks might be a more accurate descriptor, Mister Scott."

Kirk looked over sharply at Spock's correction, and McCoy cocked an eyebrow.

"Strong words, Mister Spock. An attack suggests motive."

"As does sabotage, Doctor."

Kirk interjected before McCoy could throw Spock a barbed comment.

"Could it possibly be some outside interference? Romulan or Klingon perhaps?"

Spock shook his head.

"I have conducted wide-band scans of local space for any unusual sensor readings, transmissions or activities. As our speed is limited to impulse, this has provided strong evidence against the existence of any shadowing vessel."

Kirk exhaled slowly. Had they been at warp when the dilithium chamber malfunctioned yesterday, they'd not be sitting around this table right now. They'd not be sitting anywhere. Kirk pushed on.

"It'll take us weeks to get to Starbase Nine to complete repairs. We've been lucky so far, but there's plenty of other sensitive systems to attack."

"The thing is Jim, unless they've got some way to get off the ship, whoever's behind this would have died along with the rest of us. That would suggest either some form of chemical or psychosomatic imbalance or one hell of a grudge."

Spock nodded at McCoy's brutally honest appraisal, his voice in calm contrast to the anger Kirk felt at his crew and ship being threatened.

"IT'S SETTLED THEN. WE HAVE A SABOTEUR ON BOARD MY SHIP."

"Agreed. I would recommend an immediate review of the crew's psychological profiles, Doctor."

"Good idea Spock. I'll get Chapel and M'Benga to assist. We'll start with newly rotated crew and work backwards."

"A logical approach."

Mr Scott leaned forward, spreading his hands out on the smooth wooden table. Kirk noticed it wasn't dirt on his fingers, but scorch marks. He knew the engineer had only just averted a chamber overload but didn't realize he'd burned himself in the process.

"Like I said, Captain, they'd need a high level of technical knowledge and all the regular engineering team have been with me for months. I canna see it's any of them."

Kirk saw Spock's brow furrow.

"What's on your mind Spock?"

"We are assuming the knowledge required to sabotage the ship requires

the individual to be an active member of the engineering crew. Given the frequent departmental rotations of lower ranked crewmembers within Starfleet, would it not be possible for someone to possess the requisite information from a different specialism?"

Everyone turned to the engineer. He opened his mouth to speak, when the room was flooded with a deep scarlet light.

*　*　*

As soon as Kirk exited the turbolift doors and heard the calm voice of the computer counting down, and knew the starship's self-destruct sequence had been activated.

Striding over to the science station with Spock, the Vulcan engaged the tie-in for Kirk's voice command.

"Computer. Code one two three continuity, abort destruct order."

"Code incorrect."

Kirk nodded to Spock, who repeated the command.

"Code incorrect."

"Fascinating."

Kirk sucked in a breath and looked over to the numbers on Spock's screen. Twelve minutes. Now they *were* in trouble.

"Spock, see what you can do.

Uhura – mute the audio countdown."

Spock nodded over to Chekov and Sulu who opened the panels beneath the helm to reveal winking lights and snaking cables then got to work on his own station. Kirk headed over to Scott's vacant bridge position and punched the communication button to engineering.

"Mr Scott… report."

Kirk could hear frantic shouting and movement in the background.

"We're doing what we can sir, but we're locked out of the warp core ejection system. I canna prevent the self-destruct."

"Get your team out of there. We'll evacuate the ship."

Mr Scott paused. Kirk's heart sank.

"The pressurization circuits to the lifeboats and the shuttlebay have been cut. I've got teams working on them now."

Kirk clenched his fist in frustration.

"How long Mr Scott?"

"I canna say sir. We have to find the damage first."

"Do what you can. Kirk out."

Kirk punched the comms button and leaned onto his arms, mind racing. Ten minutes to go, with no way to stop the *Enterprise* destroying itself or to abandon ship. At least the

Kobayashi Maru presented options. Kirk's thoughts were interrupted by the swooshing of the bridge doors. McCoy barreled towards Spock's station waving a library tape in his hand.

"I think I've got our man, Jim."

Kirk joined McCoy as the Vulcan rose to his feet who, with a brief shake of the head, confirmed he'd not been able to override the self-destruct. McCoy pushed the red rectangular card into the library reader, and the image of a thirty-something man flickered into view on one of Spock's screens.

"Lieutenant Horst Renner. He's a sensor specialist, shipped in a few weeks back to help with the environmental system's maintenance."

Kirk had met Renner shortly after he came aboard; intense, serious and driven, just the kind of person Kirk wanted aboard his ship. Or so he thought.

"Why do you think he's the saboteur?"

McCoy flicked a couple of switches on Spock's station, replacing Renner's face with scrolling text.

"First thing that concerned me was his psych test positivity bias. It's the strongest mark I've ever seen, nearly off the scale. This made me dig a little deeper into his medical history. On the face of it, the score

"THERE'S YOUR MOTIVE, CAPTAIN. GOOD OLD-FASHIONED REVENGE."

is a reaction to a long period of intensive counseling he received after the death of his partner on his previous posting."

The hairs on the back of Kirk's neck began to rise. From the look on McCoy's face, he wasn't going to like what was coming.

"It was the *U.S.S. Lexington,* where he served as a duotronics specialist before -"

"Before the M-5 multitronic unit took control of the *Enterprise* and killed fifty-three of her crew."

Spock raised an eyebrow as he responded.

"His duties on the *Lexington* would have given him the knowledge he required to conduct the attacks we have experienced. As Engineer Scott proposed, the saboteur would need to know the *Enterprise* extensively. The *Lexington* is also a Constitution Class vessel, making its systems virtually identical."

Kirk thought back to those dreadful hours on Stardate 4729.4 when Daystrom's computer had run

amok, badly damaging the *Lexington* and killing the entire crew of the *Excalibur* when it mistook battle simulations for the real thing.

"There's your motive, Captain. Good old-fashioned revenge."

Kirk glanced at the countdown. Six minutes to go.

"Uhura… where's Lieutenant Renner's quarters?"

Uhura checked her intra-ship transmission logs.

"Deck Five, Captain."

* * *

Kirk arrived at Renner's quarters in sixty seconds, but it was a minute he didn't have. As he approached, he was surprised – and immediately wary – when the doors slid open.

"Bones… tell security to stand fast when they get here. Let me speak with him."

McCoy glanced into the quarters and nodded.

"I've prepared a shot in case we need it. Good luck, Jim."

Just before he entered, Kirk turned back to McCoy.

"What was Renner's partner called?"

"Sarah… Sarah Reilly."

Kirk nodded then walked into the main living area to find Renner sitting at his workstation, staring at an old-fashioned photograph of a smiling woman on the desk.

"Renner. Are you responsible for the attacks on my ship?"

Renner didn't turn as he responded in a flat voice.

"Yes, Captain. I am."

Kirk moved to face Renner and looked down at his vacantly staring face.

"I… understand why you might feel – "

Renner's head snapped upwards, his face twisted with fury.

"You *understand*? Did you *understand* when you let a machine kill my partner on the *Lexington*? Kill my friends?"

Kirk felt his own long-suppressed emotions thunder back. He'd had some low points in his career, but M-5 held special pain.

"I did everything I could to prevent it. Not a day goes by I don't regret having that damned thing on the *Enterprise*."

Renner rose to his feet, shaking visibly. Kirk could see he'd lost control.

"This precious ship of yours murdered everyone I ever cared about, Captain, so now I'm going to kill it."

McCoy hissed from the doorway.

"Jim... we've only got four minutes left. I can – "

"Stay where you are Doctor. This is between me and Renner."

Kirk could see the grief in Renner's eyes. The pain had been festering, consuming all reason and controlling his every waking moment. Hopefully, there was something left of his humanity for Kirk to appeal to.

"Renner, if you want to blame anyone, blame me. I could have protested, had Daystrom and M-5 moved onto another ship, but I allowed it to happen. It was a machine who was responsible for the death of your partner, not the Enterprise – or her crew."

Renner winced at the mention of his partner and the crew.

"It *was* the *Enterprise* that took her away from me."

Something occurred to Kirk. Renner understood circuits and processors, algorithms and programs. That might be the angle to take.

"M-5 was an imperfect device created by an unstable man. It wasn't any of the souls aboard this ship, who you've lived and worked with. They weren't even on board. How is killing them going to serve your revenge, or bring Sarah back?"

Renner staggered back a couple of steps at the sound of his partner's name.

"A flawed... machine..."

Kirk seized his opportunity.

"You know better than anyone that computers are only as good as the information you give them Renner. There's no blame to be found within my crew."

"Jim – we're down to the last minute!"

Kirk held a warning hand out to McCoy, then stepped around the desk

and grabbed Renner's shoulders. He gazed into Renner's exhausted eyes.

"Stop the countdown, before M5's faulty programming claims another four hundred innocent victims. I'm sure Sarah wouldn't have wanted any of this."

Renner looked down to the photograph, the hint of a smile on his lips.

"No... she wouldn't..."

Renner pushed the comms button on his monitor.

"Computer. Code seven seven seven *Lexington*, abort destruct order."

"Destruct sequence aborted."

The security team ran into Renner's quarters and flanked the broken man as McCoy followed them in and spoke to the redshirts.

"Take him to sickbay. Gently."

McCoy nodded to Kirk then followed the guards out, leaving Kirk to pick up the photograph.

It would be a long road back for Renner, if he ever truly recovered, but Kirk was sure this was the best place in Starfleet to help him on his journey.

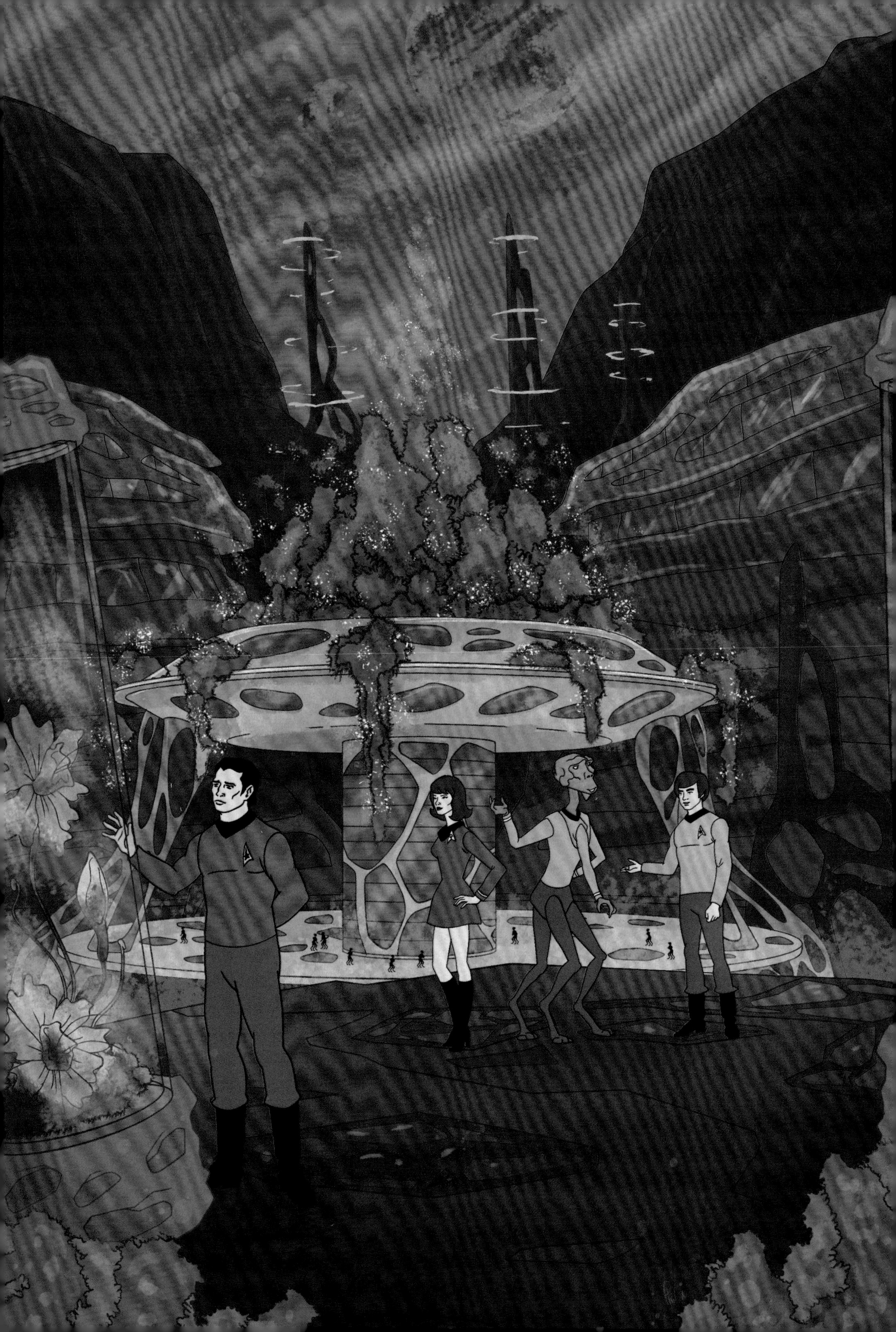

Forewarned and Three-Armed

STORY: RICH HANDLEY

OPENING ILLUSTRATION: PHILIP MURPHY

EDOS HOMEWORLD ILLUSTRATION: AARON HARVEY

 avigator's Personal Log: It's been years since my last visit to Edos, and as I ease the U.S.S. Enterprise into orbit, I'm apprehensive. I was the outsider, the quiet wanderer, which drove me away from Edos and into the merchant space fleet. Even with two dozen siblings I was like an only child, always lonely in our crowded home. But my world may be in danger, and I will do what I always do: my duty."

Arex Na Eth galumphed. The *U.S.S. Enterprise* had been dispatched to Edos to investigate a possible assassination attempt. Captain Kirk had chosen the lieutenant to lead the landing party, and so he found himself in the Edosian government hall once more. He understood why it had fallen to him – this was, after all, Arex's homeworld. Nonetheless, the assignment made him uncomfortable, like suckerfish compressed in a fishery web.

Arex considered his assigned team. He'd worked alongside Hikaru Sulu ever since Pavel Chekov's transfer to security had led to Arex's bridge posting. And he was grateful for the chance to work with Chekov, his former navigation student at Starfleet Academy. The others in the landing party were Anne Nored, Chekov's security mentor, and Dawson Walking Bear, recently promoted to lieutenant for his role in ending the Kukulkan threat. All four were among the *Enterprise*'s finest.

"Are you nervous?" asked Walking Bear. The two had been close ever since bunking together aboard the ill-fated *U.S.S. Fontana*, and Dawson knew his moods.

"Nervous like the *Bonaventure* crew during first warp," Arex admitted.

"Well, technically Zefram Cochrane's ship did that, not the *Bonaventure*," his friend corrected. "A lot of people get that wrong. One of my Comanche ancestors helped to build the *Phoenix*, you know."

Arex chuckled. He did, in fact, know. Dawson mentioned it often.

"Yes, but the *Bonaventure* was the greater ship," Chekov interjected. "It was invented by Russians. Sturdier construction, superior engineering."

Arex knew better than to get pulled into a debate between two heritage-proud shipmates. "We'd better go in," he said in his melodic, high-pitched voice, then pressed his middle hand to a recognition plate, causing the chamber door to enter.

*   *   *

Orip Ban Recoro rose with a grimace. Her right leg was bandaged, causing her to favor the other pair, and two arms were immobilized in slings. "Arex, how lovely to see you," Orip beamed. "You have been too long gone from your people, and from your family."

"It's good to see you as well, Peace Minister," Arex replied. The politician, his father's lifelong friend, had known Arex since the latter's childhood, but such familiarity in front of his colleagues made him self-conscious. He changed the subject. "You're recovering well from the accident. I'm glad."

"This was no accident, Arex," Orip replied, a slight edginess coloring her dulcet tone. "As I told the Federation government, that pilot deliberately scuttled the ship. I am sure of it. His eyes were so cold. He didn't even flinch as we hit the ground."

"If there was foul play here, Minister, we'll find it," Arex assured his elder.

"With no disrespect, Minister Orip, I am not convinced this was deliberate," Chekov chimed in. "Lieutenant Sutherland was a decorated Starfleet officer. I cannot help but wonder why he would wish to kill you."

"Maybe that wasn't really Sutherland," Nored mused. "Could have been an impostor." Arex knew Anne was not speculating idly, for a Vendorian shapeshifter had once taken the form of her late fiancé, Carter Winston.

"Nored's right, Arex," Sulu said, "something doesn't add up. We don't even know what killed Sutherland. The reports said his body had no detectable damage after the crash. He just… wasn't alive. Doctor McCoy should run an autopsy."

Arex thought for a moment, then replied, "Agreed. If you don't object, Minister…?"

"Not at all," Orip said. "We stored the pilot in the stasis room for our ancestors, knowing you'd want to examine him." She led the way, explaining to the others, "We honor those who came before. Our legacy is immortalized on the lower decks."

A tripped alarm sounded, and the team sprinted the rest of the way. They interrupted a pair of men removing the pilot's corpse from stasis. Both wore Starfleet uniforms, and at the sight of the new arrivals, one pulled out a disruptor weapon and fired wildly.

The first shot missed Walking Bear's ear by a centimeter, the other burning a gash in Chekov's calf. Pavel let out an agonized yell as Walking Bear dove behind a console, returning fire. The shooter hit the floor, unconscious.

The other intruder held his ground, firing off several shots from behind the stasis tube, but he was outgunned.

Phasers drawn, Nored and a limping Chekov shielded Minister Orip as she crouched behind a sarcophagus. With the security officers providing cover fire, Sulu and Arex moved in from opposite angles, somersaulting their way across the room to avoid being picked off.

A stray shot hit Sutherland's corpse, causing it to spark and smoke. "What the…?" Sulu said in surprise. "He's a machine!"

Arex propelled himself at the room's climate controls, keying in authorization. "Activate life-support belts!" he ordered. Nored, lacking a spare belt, pulled Orip close and wrapped her own around both their wrists, extending the energy field to encompass the minister as well. Arex lowered the room's temperature by a hundred degrees, then boosted the airflow strength to maximum.

> "LIEUTENANT SUTHERLAND WAS A DECORATED STARFLEET OFFICER. I CANNOT HELP BUT WONDER WHY HE WOULD WISH TO KILL YOU."

aaron harvey

The sudden blast of freezing air staggered the second shooter, and Sulu disarmed him with a double-kick to the hand and abdomen. Arex grabbed the gasping would-be body thief by the throat, using his middle arm. "Who are you?" he demanded. "Why the robot? And what's your purpose on Edos?"

"We had orders from Starfleet," the shivering captive sneered.

"Nonsense," Chekov said through gritted jaws. "You are *not* with Starfleet, and you'll have more than 'orders' to deal with if you don't tell us what you know."

"That'll do, Ensign," Nored said, then yanked the suspect's arm behind his back with surprising strength for someone her size. "He's right, though. I spent four months on a high-gravity world. I don't advise you resist." The prisoner's painful wince punctuated her warning, and he went slack.

"Let's get back to the *Enterprise*," Arex said, normalizing the climate controls. "Nored and Walking Bear, take Mr. Starfleet here and his sleeping friend into custody. We'll question him in sickbay while the doctor makes sure Anne didn't dislocate his shoulder."

"Aye, sir," she replied, pulling out her communicator. "*Enterprise*, seven to beam up. Have Doctor McCoy and Lieutenant Gabler stand by to receive a stasis tube."

"Understood, mrraaow," purred Shiboline M'Ress, one of the starship's relief communications officers. The Caitian relayed Nored's instructions to the crew.

Arex faced his family friend. "I'll have guards beamed down to keep you safe, Minister Orip," he promised. She gratefully squeezed Arex's arm. He

gestured toward Chekov's wound, noting, "You'd better give Pavel a hand, Hikaru."

Sulu helped the singed ensign stand. "Actually, I could use a foot," Chekov quipped. He noticed his Comanche shipmate struggling with the unconscious shooter, and added, "Like Dawson, I am walking barely."

Nored laughed, and as the transporter whine began, Walking Bear responded, "Oh, har har. I guess the one thing Russians never 'invented' was humor."

Pavel grinned through the pain, and Sulu chuckled, saying, "What I wouldn't give right now for a Slaver weapon."

*   *   *

Anne Nored stood guard over the captives in sickbay, while Randi Bryce, a recent transfer from the *U.S.S. Ariel*, tended to Chekov's injury.

"Jim, this man is a Klingon," Leonard McCoy proclaimed, waving a hand scanner over the suspect strapped to one diagnostic bed. "So's he," he said of the phaser-stunned accomplice. "And *that* one," he indicated the stasis tube, "is an android."

"A Klingon…" Captain James T. Kirk considered McCoy's words, cocking an eyebrow at his friend. "I'm pretty sure you've used that line before, Bones. You're repeating yourself in your old age."

"I'm a medical doctor, not a script doctor," McCoy grumbled. "Besides, it's not my fault some Klingons look human. Without their damn ridges,

they can infiltrate us any time they like. Starfleet should have listened when I suggested keeping safe tribbles handy on every ship. A tribble a day keeps the Klingon away. Just ask Arne Darvin."

"Works better than apples, I suppose," Kirk admitted. "Just don't give Cyrano Jones any ideas. There aren't enough glommers in the universe." He looked the defiant prisoner up and down. "As for you… tell me why the Empire is so interested in Edosians."

The suspect snarled, "I am Kroma, proud warrior of the House of Kuri! There is nothing you can do or say to loosen my tongue. I have braved the fiery –" He stopped, then less confidently asked, "Did he say tribbles?"

Kirk exchanged glances with McCoy. "We… only use them as a last resort," he said.

"You would subject a prisoner to such vile vermin?" the Klingon asked uncertainly. "I thought Starfleet didn't allow torture."

"We do what we must," Kirk replied with a shrug, "though we find it distasteful."

"And you keep *tribbles* on your starship?"

"These aren't ordinary tribbles, mind you," McCoy said, exaggerating his drawl. "These are *colony* tribbles. Genetically engineered, the size of a room, utterly terrifying. They're disease and danger, wrapped in darkness and silence."

"And they're pink," Arex added.

"And they're *pink*!" McCoy reiterated.

"They're adorable," Nored joined in. "*So* much cooing. You're gonna love 'em."

"Great Kahless, you humans are deranged!" Kroma sputtered. "Fine, keep those filthy fur sacks away and I'll tell you what you want to know. When I am done here, I will tear the

ample meat from the rotting corpse of that *forshak* Harry Mudd! He said his androids were foolproof, but the first one short-circuited before carrying out its damn mission." He grunted and spat. "Swapping out bodies isn't worthy of a Klingon. Making robots, skulking around, wearing gaudy costumes, acting like *scientists* – feh!"

Kirk's eyes widened. "Did you say… Harry Mudd?"

* * *

Orip Ban Recoro stared blankly. "Who?"

"Harcourt Fenton Mudd," Kirk clarified, turning the viewscreen to display Harry's record. "A scoundrel, scam artist, conman, and unrepentant reprobate. Oddly likable, though. Most recently, we caught him peddling love crystals on Motherlode. That caused… well, let's say a rise in hormone levels throughout the ship which have since made things…

uncomfortable for a lot of my crew."

Arex fidgeted. He still couldn't look Charlene Masters in the eye.

"And why does this Mudd person want me dead?" Orip asked.

"In truth," Kirk continued. "we're not sure whether Harry was involved at all, beyond selling the Empire some ancient tech from an android planet. It's… the Klingons who were trying to kill you."

The ungulate peace minister's face furrowed. "For what purpose?"

"According to our talkative friend Kroma, the Empire had their eye on a certain herbaceous plant native to your world. They wanted your flowers, Minister."

The elder blinked, her greyish-orange skin darkening in hue. "Flowers?"

"Edosian orchids," Arex interjected. "The poison is an excruciating assassination tool. I saw firsthand on the *Fontana* how brutal Klingons can be."

"I'M PRETTY SURE YOU'VE USED THAT LINE BEFORE, BONES. YOU'RE REPEATING YOURSELF IN YOUR OLD AGE."

The peace minister nodded comprehendingly. "I see. But all of *this* for *flowers*?"

"Not just the orchids," Arex corrected her. "They wanted the whole planet."

"The Empire reverse-engineered the androids," Kirk said, "with the goal of galactic subjugation. One posed as Sutherland to replace you with an Edosian model, but after the short-circuit caused him to crash, the Klingons needed to hide the evidence."

"Hence, the fake uniforms," Arex added. "If they were caught, Starfleet would be implicated in your murder."

"So Chekov was right," she mused. "The crash *was* an accident."

"Yes, but the danger was real. The Empire would have infiltrated one world after another," Kirk added. "Edos today, Pandro or Mantilles tomorrow. With no shots fired and no one aware it was happening."

"It all sounds so ridiculously... cartoonish," Orip said.

"Aboard the *Enterprise*," Arex stated, "the ridiculous is often reality. On one mission, we all turned into infants. On another, we were all shrunken to a few inches in height."

"My stars!" the peace minister exclaimed.

"Then there was the scientist who cloned Spock as a giant to... help talking plants make the galaxy happier," Kirk recalled. "Spock also lost his brain once. That was surreal."

Orip's eyes darted from one officer to the other. "Did those things really happen?"

"It's been a strange few years," Arex admitted.

"Astounding," she said, shaking her head. "You live a fascinating life, Arex, and Edos is proud. I'm sure your family would enjoy hearing about it."

"Ah, yes, well," Arex stammered, his voice squeaking, "I don't think there's time for a visit. The ship is due... erm, somewhere."

"Not at all, Mister Arex," Kirk said, his mouth curling wryly at one corner. "We've got *plenty* of time before we leave orbit."

"I appreciate that, Captain, but that won't be neces –"

"Go see your family, Lieutenant. The *Enterprise* can wait."

"But, sir –"

"That's an order."

"Yes, sir," Arex said meekly. "Thank you, sir."

Orip grinned. "Bring your sessica. You know your mother loves to hear you play."

"Good idea," Arex whimpered glumly.

"It's settled," Kirk said. "Ensign Harvey can beam down anything you need. Have a wonderful reunion, Arex. It sounds... fun."

"Edosian reunions are more than fun, Captain," Orip said, a gleam in her eye. "They're downright animated."

Working Miracles

STORY: BY JAKE BLACK
ILLUSTRATION: PETE WALLBANK

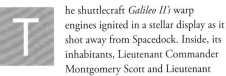

The shuttlecraft *Galileo II's* warp engines ignited in a stellar display as it shot away from Spacedock. Inside, its inhabitants, Lieutenant Commander Montgomery Scott and Lieutenant Nyota Uhura, manned the controls, setting a course for the Suhazal system and their rendezvous with the *U.S.S. Enterprise.*

"It'll be good to be home," Scotty said.

"What? Don't tell me you didn't love every minute of that conference," Uhura laughed.

The two friends had spent the last week at a gathering of Starfleet's finest operations officers, seeing for the first time the initial designs for the *Constitution*-class refit. With the *Enterprise* due to complete her five-year mission in three months, it was essential that Scotty and Uhura, as the ship's senior operations officers, be briefed on the new systems.

"Aye, lassie, I suppose you're right. The refit *Enterprise* is going to be a beauty of a ship," Scotty sighed. "I just want to see her one more time before they tear her apart and put her back together."

Uhura patted Scotty's back as she moved to the aft of the shuttle, pulling ration packs from a storage compartment.

"Well, the communications systems upgrades look very impressive. The Golding brothers gave quite the presentation," she said, handing Scotty one of the packs. "And you couldn't have asked for a more appropriate venue than the Ames Research Center."

Scotty smiled and set his ration pack on the console. "That three-hundred-year-old building has seen better days. But I guess if it was a good enough place to design the six *Voyager* probes and the first Mars rover missions, it's good enough for the *Enterprise,*" he said with a glint in his eye.

They each tore the silver packaging from their ration packs.

"Nothing like a starlit dinner," Uhura joked.

"With good company," Scotty replied.

Suddenly, the shuttlecraft jerked to a stop, sending Scotty and Uhura, and their meals, crashing

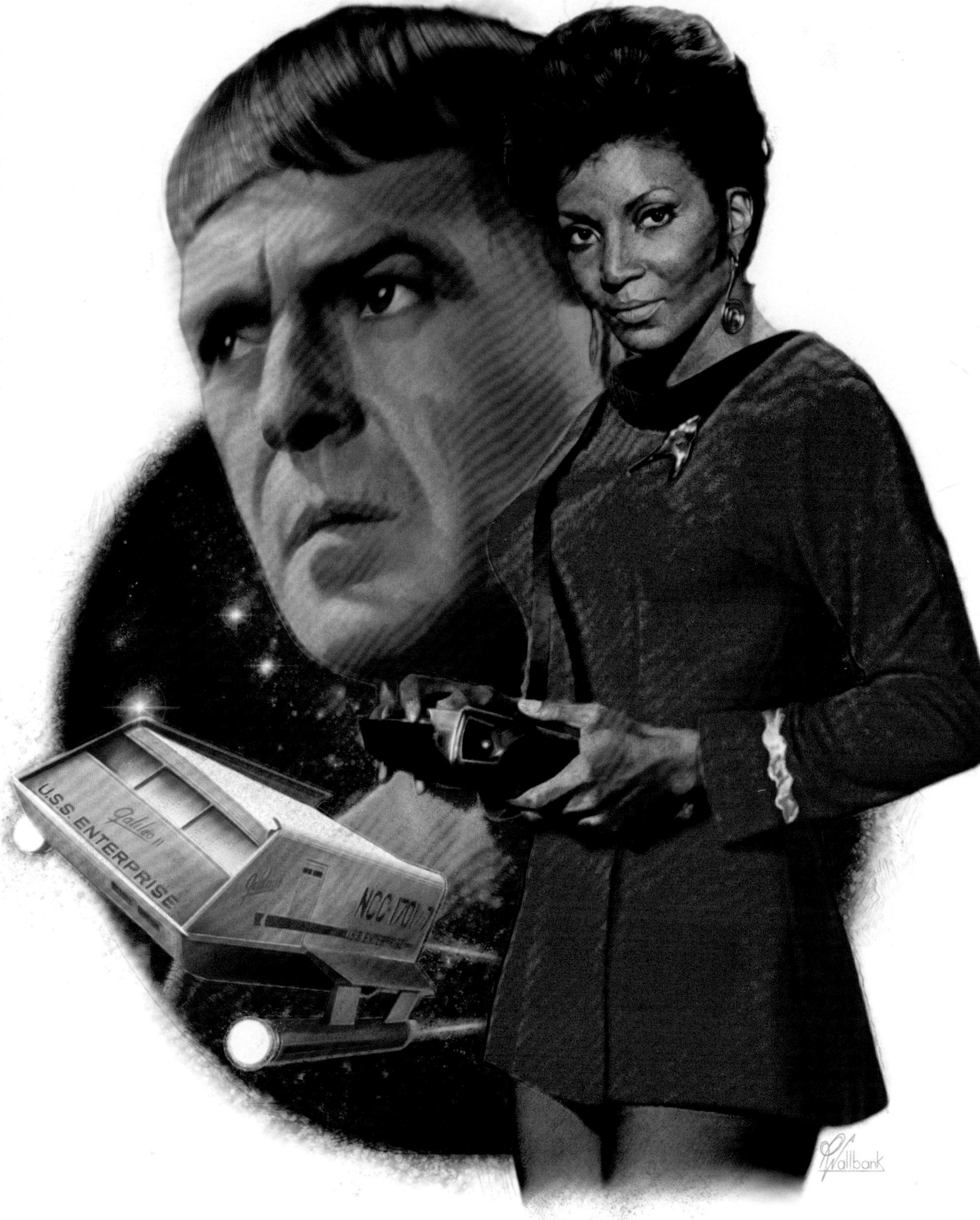
U.S.S. ENTERPRISE
Wallbank

"WE'RE BEING PULLED BY A TRACTOR BEAM!"

to floor. Scotty leapt to his feet and studied the console.

"We're being pulled by a tractor beam!" he shouted.

The *Galileo* was dragged toward a massive freighter, that displayed no name and no affiliation.

"Unidentified vessel, this is the Shuttlecraft *Galileo*. You have committed an act of aggression against the Federation. We demand you release us immediately," Uhura said into the shuttlecraft's comms relay.

"No reply," Uhura said, slapping the console as Scotty feverishly, albeit futilely, tried to break the shuttle free.

"Their tractor beam is strong! I can't warp us away, or else it would tear

the shuttle apart," Scotty said, concern hanging over his words.

Within minutes, the shuttle landed in the freighter's hanger bay. As the two *Enterprise* officers disembarked, they were met by a tall Andorian, a mammoth Ursinoid, and a phaser-wielding Orion.

Scotty took a step toward their captor, "I'm Lieutenant Commander Montgomery Scott of the Starfleet vessel *U.S.S. Ent*–

"I know who you are," the Orion sneered. "But I suppose some introductions are in order. I am Nyren, the captain of this vessel."

"I'm Scham," the Andorian said, and then, motioning to the Ursinoid, "And this is Ju-aire."

"Think of us as an association of galactic neighbors, offering… protection… to those around us," Nyren said, an eerie calm in his voice.

"You're *gangsters*!" Scotty blurted out.

"What do you want with us?" Uhura demanded.

Ju-aire let out a quiet growl as Nyren circled the Starfleet officers.

"Well, you see, this vessel is in need of repair. Its warp engines no longer function, and if we're going to continue *protecting* people, we need our ship to fly," Nyren said, licking his lips.

Scotty and Uhura shared a nervous glance as Nyren continued, "That's where you come in, Lieutenant Commander Montgomery Scott of the *U.S.S.*

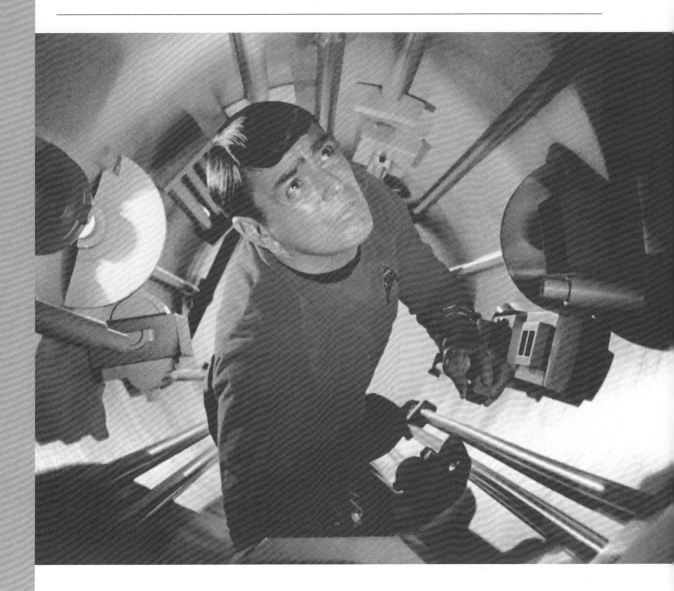

Enterprise. You're going to fix these engines."

"I'll do no such thing," Scotty defiantly exclaimed.

"Oh, you will. Or you'll die. But not just you. Her, too," Nyren whispered.

*   *   *

Engineering was eerily quiet. Scotty lay under a console, examining the inoperable engines.

"I've never seen a mish mash like this," Scotty groused. "It's like they've taken engine parts from the least advanced cultures and forced them together like pieces from a dozen different jigsaw puzzles!"

Tense, Uhura asked, "But can you fix them?"

Scotty pulled himself out and up from the console. Before he could respond, Nyren, Scham, and Ju-aire arrived.

"He'd better," Nyren answered.

Scotty stepped up to Nyren, determined. His brow furrowed, his eyes intense, he said, "No. They're unfixable. But you knew that already, didn't you? You've got an Algolian matter reactant injector tied to a Phylosian antimatter injector! It's a miracle they haven't blown up, already!"

Nyren slapped Scotty across the

face. With full force, Scotty threw a retaliatory punch, but Nyren dodged. Ju-aire grabbed Scotty by the shoulders and tossed him to the floor.

"You're lying!" Nyren shouted.

"This ship is going to explode at any minute!" Scotty yelled.

"Then, I guess you better hurry," the venom in Nyren's voice sending a clear warning. "Ju-aire. Stay here and watch them."

The Ursinoid growled an acknowledgement as Nyren and Scham left. Uhura crouched down next to Scotty.

"Are they really that volatile?" she whispered, pulling her friend to his feet.

"Aye. They must've stolen

whatever parts they could from the scrap heap and hotwired them together." Scotty replied, quietly. "They're not flying, because the matter and antimatter injectors are not compatible. They probably worked for a few weeks or months when they were first put together, but the ship's safeties shut them down."

"But if the safeties worked and turned off the engines, what's the problem?" Uhura asked.

Scotty stared at the engine, his eyes fixed on the ill-fitting matter/antimatter containment connections. "There's still a bit of matter and antimatter flowing from the injectors. The parts don't connect properly, so eventually there's going to be a leak that will destroy this ship instantly. And the way these have been put

together, it's going to be soon. There's nothing I can do."

Uhura nodded an understanding and moved to the console.

"What are you doing, human?" Ju-aire roared.

"Fixing the engines," Uhura said, simply.

"What are ye —" Scotty began.

Uhura drew Scotty close and whispered, "If we can't stop this ship from exploding, we've got to get out of here. I have to contact the *Enterprise*."

Scotty stepped toward Ju-aire. "Can't ye see she's going to save all of us! Back off and give her some space!"

"Their communications systems are just as archaic as their engines," Uhura whispered. "It's like using a telegraph! But I have an idea."

Uhura's fingers strode across the

console, inputting commands and creating a coded message. As Scotty watched her work, his eyes grew wide in amazement.

"You're a genius!" Scotty said.

Moments later, Ju-aire roared, startling Uhura and Scotty. They spun around to see Nyren had returned.

"Time's almost up, Mister Scott," Nyren said. "And Ms. Uhura. For someone so adept at communications, I would've thought you'd know how sensitive an Ursinoid's hearing is. We know you're trying to send a message to the *Enterprise*."

Nyren stood face to face with Scotty and Uhura. His mouth twisting into a sinister grin.

"For that, you will die," he said.

* * *

"IF WE CAN'T STOP THIS SHIP FROM EXPLODING, WE'VE GOT TO GET OUT OF HERE. I HAVE TO CONTACT THE ENTERPRISE."

On the bridge of the *Enterprise,* Captain James T. Kirk paced around his chair, his fingers brushing the leather back and wooden arms.

"Something's wrong," Kirk said. "It's not like Scotty and Uhura to be late."

Dr. McCoy put his arm on his friend's shoulder. "I'm sure everything's alright, Jim. If I know Scotty, he is probably still talking to the Starfleet Corps of Engineers about warp manifolds, or the colors of the new plasma injectors, or some other nonsense."

"Maybe so, but my gut says it's something else," Kirk said. "Any luck with your scans, Mister Spock?"

"Luck, Captain? No. Nor has there been any other sign of the shuttle on long range sensors," Spock spoke plainly.

"Mister Spock, I may have something," Lieutenant Emily Malina said from the communications station.

Kirk moved toward her. "What is it, Lieutenant?"

"It's a coded message, I think, from Lieutenant Uhura. It's carrying the *Galileo*'s transponder signal," Malina said, "and was sent specifically to this station."

"Confirmed, Captain," Spock said. "The signal includes Lieutenant Uhura's Starfleet I.D. and contains a set of coordinates."

Kirk nodded and moved to his chair. "Mister Chekov, set a course for those coordinates. Mister Sulu, maximum warp," Kirk ordered.

"Aye, Captain," Chekov and Sulu said in unison.

* * *

Ju-aire gripped Uhura's shoulders, his claws digging into her shoulders, causing three rivers of blood to pour down each of her arms. Nyrean and Scham stood over Scotty who reworked wires and cables under the engine console.

"I'm telling you, this ship is about to blow!" Scotty protested. "The matter/antimatter injector connections are getting looser, causing a warp core breach!"

Nyren drew his phaser.

"Ju-aire, let her go," he ordered.

Ju-aire shoved Uhura toward Nyren, his phaser pointed directly at her.

"It's too bad your friend failed," Nyren screamed. "And too bad you *tried to send a message to the* Enterprise!"

As Nyren curled his finger around his phaser's trigger, the ship's computer's voice rang out, "*Warning. Proximity alert. Warning. Proximity alert.*"

"What is this?!" Nyren demanded, activating a small viewscreen near the engine console and seeing the *Enterprise* approaching.

"They're hailing us!" Scham shouted.

James T. Kirk's visage filled the viewscreen.

"*Unidentified vessel, this is Captain James T. Kirk of the* Starship Enterprise. *You are ordered to lower your shields and surrender.*"

"Never," Nyren responded.

"*You have two of my officers aboard your ship, and our sensors show you're facing a warp core breach,*" Kirk said.

"You're lying to save your officers," Nyren said. "Scham, get us out of here. Engage the warp engines!"

"No!" Scotty screamed! "If you touch them, that'll trigger the leak from the warp core breach – and we'll all die!"

Nyren pulled Scotty to his feet and shoved him toward the engine console while applying pressure on his back,

forcing him to work the controls.

"*I'd listen to the man,*" Kirk said.

"Fix them. Now," Nyren hissed.

Scotty seemingly relented and tapped several buttons on the console, saying, "Just one more thing."

"Shields down," the computer's voice declared, just as a pair of matter and antimatter atoms collided.

* * *

The *Enterprise* viewscreen lit up in a massive explosion.

"Shields up!" Captain Kirk ordered. "Sulu, get us out of here!"

Kirk pounded the controls on his chair.

"Transporter room, report," Kirk said, an anxious urgency in his voice.

"*I've got them, Captain. Mister Scott and Lieutenant Uhura, as well as their three captors,*" Lieutenant Kyle's voice echoed through the bridge.

"Security. Lieutenant Ramirez, escort our guests to the brig," Kirk said.

"*On it,*" Ramirez said.

"*Captain, Lieutenant Uhura appears injured,*" Kyle said.

"Bones," Kirk said as Dr. McCoy raced to the turbolift.

Kirk felt himself exhale for the first time in several minutes.

* * *

With Nyran, Scham, and Ju-aire held safely in the brig, and Dr. McCoy having healed Uhura's injuries, Scotty found himself sitting in his quarters, contemplating the past week's events. He looked out the window, not at the stars but at the red glow from the warp nacelles. In the coming months, they would be replaced with a sleeker design. While more effective, to be sure, he didn't know if they'd be as pretty as these ones which he'd overseen for the last five years.

His sentimental thoughts were broken by his door buzzer.

"Come in," he called.

Uhura stepped in, her hands behind her back.

"I hope I'm not interrupting," she said.

"You? Never, lassie. Come in," Scotty replied.

"That was…quite a day…" Uhura said.

"Aye," Scotty said. "But we survived. All thanks to you."

Uhura smiled.

"I mean, using that ship's internal comms to route a message to the *Enterprise* through the shuttle! Like I said, genius!"

"Well, I'm just glad we came through it and made it home ok," Uhura said. "I have a surprise for you."

From behind her back, Uhura presented a pair of silver packaged ration packs.

"We didn't get to finish our starlit dinner," she said.

"With good company," Scotty grinned. ⋆

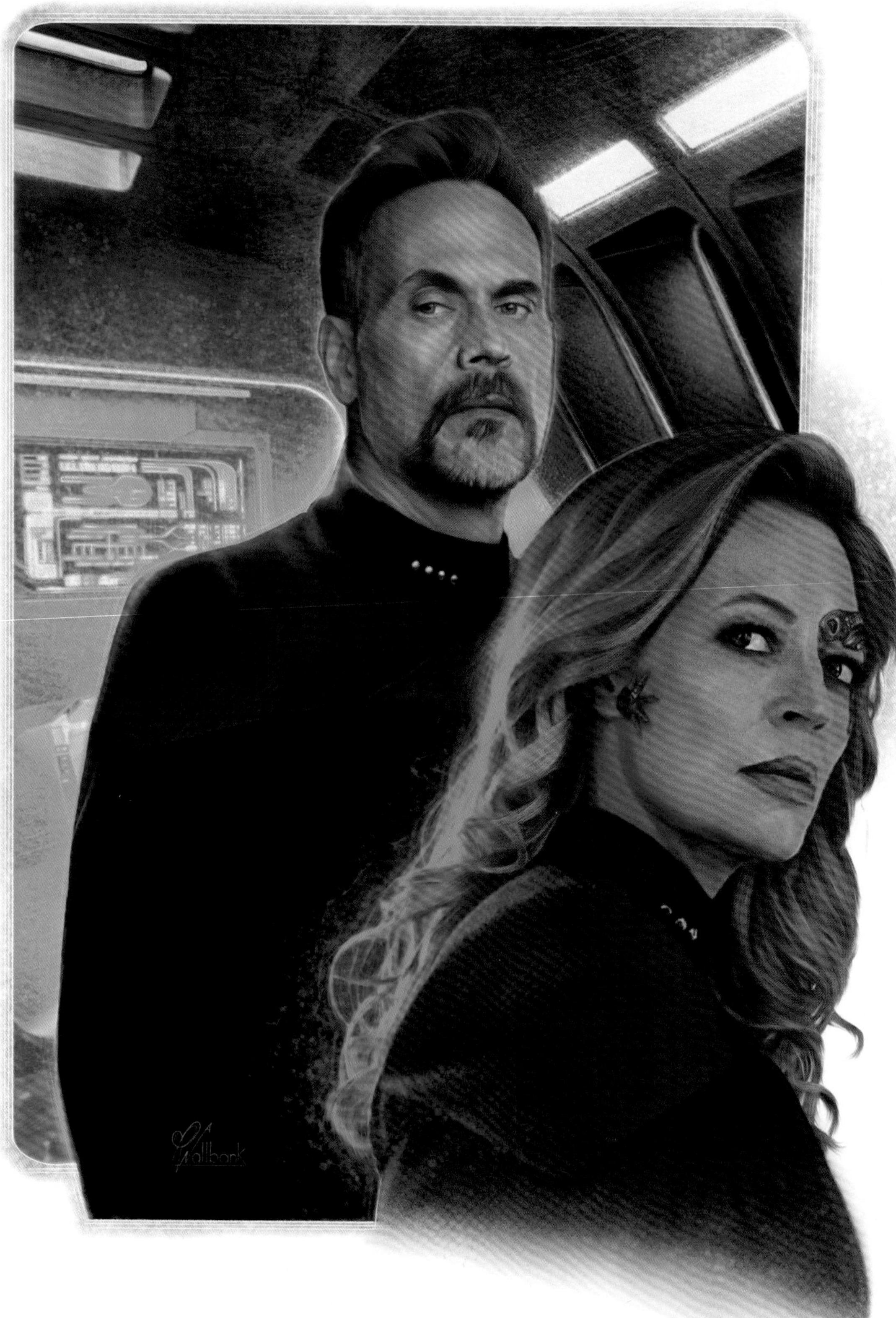

Confirmation Bias

STORY: MICHAEL DISMUKE
ILLUSTRATION: PETE WALLBANK

"Your vessel will be towed to Starbase G-6 where you'll be remanded into the custody of Starfleet Security. From there, a formal tribunal will be formed to decide your fate. If your planet has a judicial system, they have the right to provide for your legal defense. Of course, they might disavow you. I would, since you are such abject losers. If that happens, you'll be provided a representative from our judge advocate general's office."

Liam Shaw, captain of the *U.S.S. Titan*-A, finished reading the two captives their rights.

The Usangi'i males sat in two separate but adjacent holding cells in the ship's brig. Blue-hued force fields prevented the duo of criminals from escaping. Shaw couldn't help but think that the portly prisoners, dressed in shiny orange uniforms, resembled tubby worms with the facial features of star-nosed moles – the kind he had caught as a kid back home in Illinois. In a universe shaped by the peculiarities of interstellar evolution, the faces of the Usangi'i captives looked as if a cosmic engineer had attached an otherworldly satellite dish to their snouts. Comprising thirty to forty fleshy, prehensile tendrils that splayed outward like a miniature constellation, their unique facial appendages were endowed with hyper-sensitive neural clusters. These clusters resembled minuscule antenna arrays, fine-tuned to intercept and interpret environmental signals.

The crew of the *Titan*-A would have preferred to learn about a new, sentient species in a more diplomatic manner. However, the actions of the Usangi'i had changed their status to that of prisoners in the brig rather than of guests on the bridge.

"I'll make sure my chief of security sends you a few holopics of the innards of a Federation penal colony. I'd hate to keep you in suspense regarding your new digs." Captain Shaw punched a few more notes into the PADD, signed off on the formal charges, then handed it to his first officer. "How many hours until we arrive at G-6, Commander Hansen?"

Seven checked the PADD, added her own sign off, and handed it to one of the two stern-faced security officers that stood guard. "Twelve hours, sir," she responded, silently roiling at the fact that Captain Shaw refused to refer to her by her chosen name.

Though she had thrown off the shackles of the Borg Collective, she had spent approximately half of her life as Seven of Nine, Tertiary Adjunct of Unimatrix Zero One. Once liberated from the Borg, her crewmates aboard *U.S.S. Voyager* called her by the abbreviated moniker "Seven of Nine" – or just "Seven" – as did her associates in the Fenris Rangers. Shaw's insistence on referring to her by her birth name, Annika Hansen, ran deeper than mere accuracy and formality, though the man was a model of procedural compliance. Over the course of weeks, the tonal inflections with which he uttered her name evolved from passive-aggressive jabs to more overt microaggressions.

"Captain," Seven asked as they exited the brig into the bustling corridor of the *Neo-Constitution*-class ship, "may we speak privately?"

"I don't see why not," he responded without making eye contact.

Within short order, Shaw and Seven regrouped to the starship's Observation Lounge.

Shaw rounded the conference table and sat down opposite from where Seven stood. He didn't bother to offer a seat to his first officer. With a swipe of the hand, he activated the computer built into the surface of the table and tapped away without looking up. "What can I do for you, Commander Hansen?" He swiped left, making a few selections on the console.

Seven's lips pursed momentarily in a silent symphony of agitation as the captain summoned from the ship's database Vivaldi's *Concerto For Violin And Strings In F Minor*. "I would like to address what transpired during our recent contact with the Usangi'i pirates, sir."

Shaw adjusted the volume of the music to his liking. "What exactly would you like to address?" He sat back, his eyes set for the challenge. "We made first contact with a new species. We quickly determined hostile intent. We uncovered their ruse. Now they sit in the brig awaiting Starfleet justice. Not bad for this crew's thirty-fifth mission. If you want to take the lead in writing the report, go right ahead."

"I'm not sure you want me to write that report." She offered a moment's hesitation. "Sir."

"Is that so?" The challenge had been accepted. He leaned forward, locking his hands together and resting his elbows on the table. "Pray tell."

Seven's brain sifted through many unsuitable responses. Years of outspokenness, tempered by a crash course in command officer training at Starfleet Academy, had taught her that her candidness could upset colleagues. Balancing diplomacy and honesty was challenging. However, frustrated by her recent weeks as the *Titan's* XO, she questioned her future in Starfleet. "Permission to speak freely, Captain."

Shaw's eyes narrowed and he gave a cautious tilt of his head. "Go right ahead."

"At 0515 hours, *Titan's* sensors detected a subspace distress call from an unidentified vessel in the Rimall system," Seven stated, blocking out the music that permeated the Lounge. "At 0518, alpha shift arrived on the bridge wherein you ordered long-range scans of the vessel. That was at 0520 hours. Scans revealed that the unknown vessel was suffering from catastrophic engine failure. Life support was also failing. You ordered Ensign Esmar to hail the vessel. Two males identifying themselves as the last of the Usangi'i race answered the hail and requested immediate evacuation to our vessel. They stated that they were transporting the last of their species' egg banks and that their ship was seconds away from an imminent warp core breach. They further claimed that their civilization had been assimilated by the Borg."

"I was there, Commander. Get to your point," Shaw demanded.

"At 0523 hours, you ordered Ensign LaForge to close distance with the Usangi'i vessel, at which point I –"

Shaw interrupted. "Informed me that you had no recollection of such a species in your Collective memory and therefore felt that we should proceed with caution." He got up from the table and moved to the replicator situated in the wall to Seven's left. He tapped on

the replicator controls. A simple glass of water appeared in a clear cylinder container. "At which point I reminded you that you have not been a Borg in over twenty-five years and your intel is outdated and irrelevant." He paused as he reached for the glass. "'Irrelevant'. Oh. I like that word."

Seven ignored the slight. "Nonetheless, I ordered Lieutenant T'Veen to perform additional scans – scans that detected anomalous readings in their engine core. I advised keeping our distance, at which point you argued that this was a – and I quote – 'First Contact mission in clear intersection with a rescue operation wherein time is of the essence'."

"Get to your point," Shaw snapped, taking a steady swig of water without removing his gaze from the ex-Borg.

"Yes, sir," she begrudgingly stated. "Upon my insistence, T'Veen enhanced *Titan's* scans. We verified that a false warp core breach reading was in fact being generated from a masked secondary computer core aboard the Usangi'i vessel."

"I then ordered a full stop, more detailed scans of the ship, and confirmed our science officer's findings," Shaw shrugged. "Their ruse was uncovered. We learned that the dastardly duo were not transporting the last of their species as they claimed. They were, in fact, transporting microscopic nanite pods genetically modified to appear as embryonic sacs."

Seven added, "Weapons that – had they been brought aboard – would have detonated, infiltrating our vessel's computer networks and putting us under full control of the Usangi'i pirates."

Shaw offered an insincere smile. "Seems to me like we're on the same page. No harm no foul. I followed all required protocols given the seemingly urgent nature of the situation…"

"Against my recommendation."

"'Recommendation' is the key word, Hansen, not 'order'. Let me remind you – in case your cortical node is on the fritz – I give the orders around here, not you."

Seven took a step toward her commanding officer, her jaw tightening. This latest insult stripped away the veneer of passive aggression she had come to expect from her captain. He made no effort to conceal his sheer disdain for her presence. Years as a Fenris Ranger resurfaced, bringing with them a contempt for authority figures that created a vitriolic atmosphere for anyone they deemed inferior. In such a toxic environment – then and now – Seven was still

expected to perform at her best.

"My warning should have been given due respect. Instead, my observations were disregarded due to your obvious contempt for the Borg. I've read your service record. I'm aware of your experience at Wolf 359. It's not a secret that you are not a fan of xBs. You stated in a report

> "LET ME REMIND YOU – IN CASE YOUR CORTICAL NODE IS ON THE FRITZ – I GIVE THE ORDERS AROUND HERE, NOT YOU."

to Starfleet Command, that – and I quote – '…there is no guarantee that the Borg Collective can ever be fully eradicated from existence. Therefore, it behooves Starfleet to maintain a wide distance from their technology including, but not limited to, their drones – past or present.' End quote." Seven let her recollection float in the

air for a moment. "That statement would include your feelings about me, wouldn't it, Captain?"

Shaw took a hefty swig of his water, rounded the table to stand opposite of Seven once more, then set the near-empty glass on the flat surface with a purposeful clank. "It seems Starfleet completely disregarded my report. So why should you care what I think? You're here, aren't you?"

"You've resigned yourself to tolerating me. But eliminating me would be more in line with your personal preference."

"Thank God that I place following orders above personal preference. I'd say I'm a model captain."

"With all due respect –" Seven worked to squeeze those four words from her mouth. "Your tone and demeanor are meant to diminish my authority with the crew. Your mere tolerance of my presence can only lead to negative outcomes. Your bias against me puts this crew in danger."

"You are being a little overdramatic," Shaw said, as he returned to a seated position behind the table.

"Am I? You didn't even offer me the dignity of a chair when we came into the Observation Lounge."

"My apologies. I thought years

of standing in alcoves made you indifferent to static postures." Shaw watched Seven's body stiffen as his insult slid across the table and hit her right in the gut. Before she could respond, he launched a second volley. "Let's be real, Commander Hansen. I think it's safe to say that you wouldn't be here but for the influence of admirals Janeway and Picard."

Seven could see that Shaw was relishing the fact that he had inflicted a wound. She recalled that she still had permission to speak freely. His mistake. "If we are 'being real', Captain, I would also postulate that you, too, would not be here were it not for the influence of the Borg."

Vivaldi's violin died out just as Seven's words dropped. Her statement caused Shaw to rise from his seated position. She persisted. "Nonetheless, no matter what events transpired in our pasts, it's now upon us to draw on our experiences to formulate the best possible solutions in the present. My association with Admiral Janeway continually *informs* my analytical

> "YOUR INSANE CURIOSITY AND FANATICAL BELIEF THAT THE GOOD GUYS ALWAYS WIN HAS TURNED YOU INTO THE BAD GUYS; AWAKENING POWERS THAT SHOULD HAVE BEEN LEFT TO SLEEP..."

abilities. Your experiences with the Borg, in this instance, crippled your ability to accept my professional assessment without prejudice."

"Commander –" Shaw growled.

Seven knew this could be her first and final opportunity to express her thoughts. "When I first joined the crew, it took you weeks to make eye contact with me instead of focusing on my ocular implant. You don't think I noticed? From the moment I first set foot on *Voyager*, I was met with sidelong looks from that ship's crew, and it's a pattern of behavior I've come to expect since returning to the Alpha Quadrant. I've learned

to understand and adjust. I never expected the same courtesy in return, particularly not from you, Captain."

"You hero types." Shaw's voice took on a gravely tone. It rumbled with the makings of an avalanche of indignation. "While ninety-nine percent of Starfleet goes about their business defending our borders, supporting the Federation, and exploring the galaxy, you egomaniacal grandstanders push the envelope of sanity, setting ablaze the tenuous utopia the rest of us are trying to maintain. Your insane curiosity and fanatical belief that the good guys always win has turned you into the

bad guys; awakening powers that should have been left to sleep; playing with dark forces best kept in the shadows; trying to get palsy-walsy with the Devil. Someone liberates a Borg, somebody you know saves the universe a couple times, and you think your luck can't run out."

Shaw hadn't noticed his voice was now several decibels higher than when he began his rant. "The rest of us don't have that luxury, Commander. The average officer doesn't just emerge unscathed from planet-shattering explosions. We lose people. We lose ourselves. And when the majority of us take risks that cost lives, we lose our commissions. You're coming down on me for not singing the praises of the few fortunate enough to dodge death? I don't plan to run out of luck on my watch. So, you can check your gut feeling at the door and fall in line. Your opinion is not of more value than anyone else that has *actually earned* their commission, so don't get offended when I don't get giddy over every suggestion you make."

"I don't think my opinion is of

any more value than the rest of the crew, Captain," Seven said through clenched teeth. "I also don't think they are of any less value either."

"Yeah? Then maybe next time you won't crack a servo when I don't bow down before your legendary intellectual prowess. Maybe you'll take your place as one of my officers and stop touting your history as a rogue, disrupting the successful uniformity of my vessel. Fall in line, Commander. *That* is a warning."

Seven offered no response. She wanted to scream. She wanted to break the shackles of Starfleet. She wanted to let the regret of joining the organization fester and transform into an impulsive declaration that she was resigning her commission. One thing held her back.

It would give Shaw pleasure.

And she was not about to do anything of the sort.

She stifled her emotions and readjusted her stance. "Permission to be dismissed, sir."

"Oh, you can count on it." Shaw took up his glass of water

and polished off the last measure as Seven did an about-face to exit. "Commander Hansen," he said, swirling the empty glass in his hand as if he was aerating a pour of wine.

Seven stopped in her tracks, her face turned away from Shaw. She closed her eyes expecting another tongue scathing.

Knowing he had her attention, Shaw said, "I hope you know this is not a conversation I *ever* want to have again. The next time you ask to speak freely, I won't grant you the same liberty." He kept his eyes locked on her, compounding his statement by slamming the glass back on the table one more time.

Seven did everything in her power not to jump at the sound of the glass hitting the table. "I would not expect that you would, sir."

Seven exited the Observation Lounge. She now knew where she and Shaw stood in relation to each other. It was more than captain and XO. They were now professional rivals. And she was not sure that this was a game she stood a chance of winning. ⬧

THRILLING ORIGINAL SHORT-FICTION

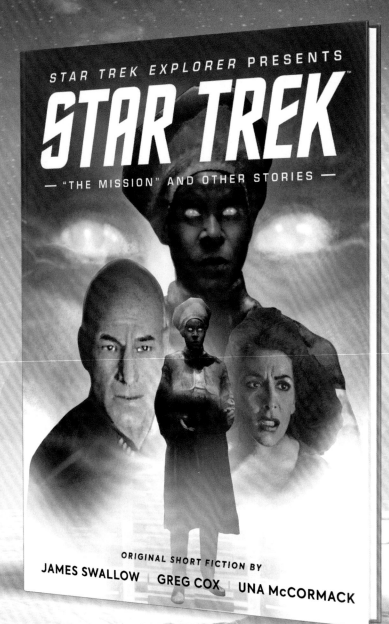

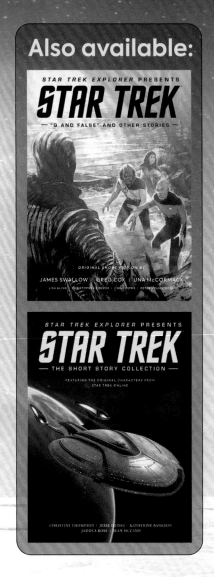

Also available:

From fan-favorite authors including:
James Swallow, Una McCormack, Lisa Klink, Paul Reed, Christine Thompson, Greg Cox, Jesse Heinig and more!

Available from all good book stores and online
TITAN-COMICS.COM

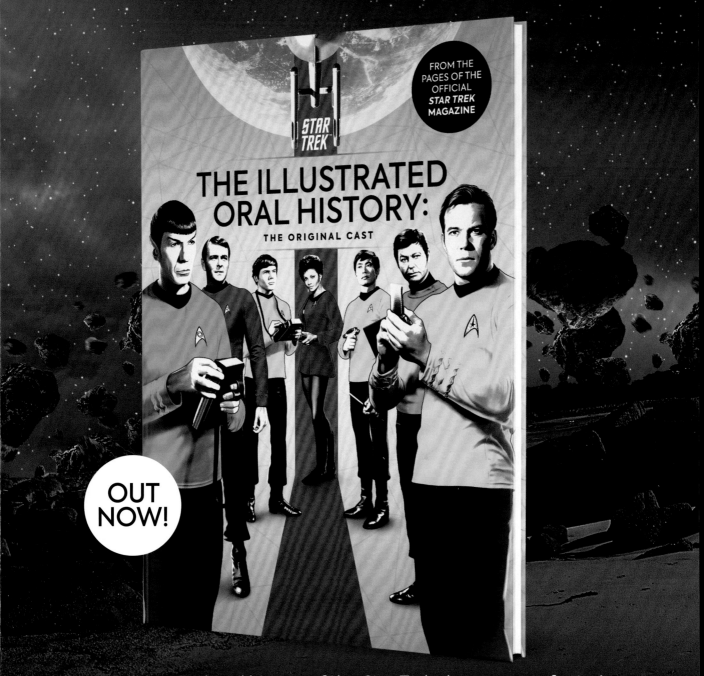

COMPLETE YOUR *STAR TREK* COLLECTION!

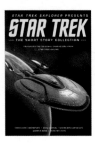

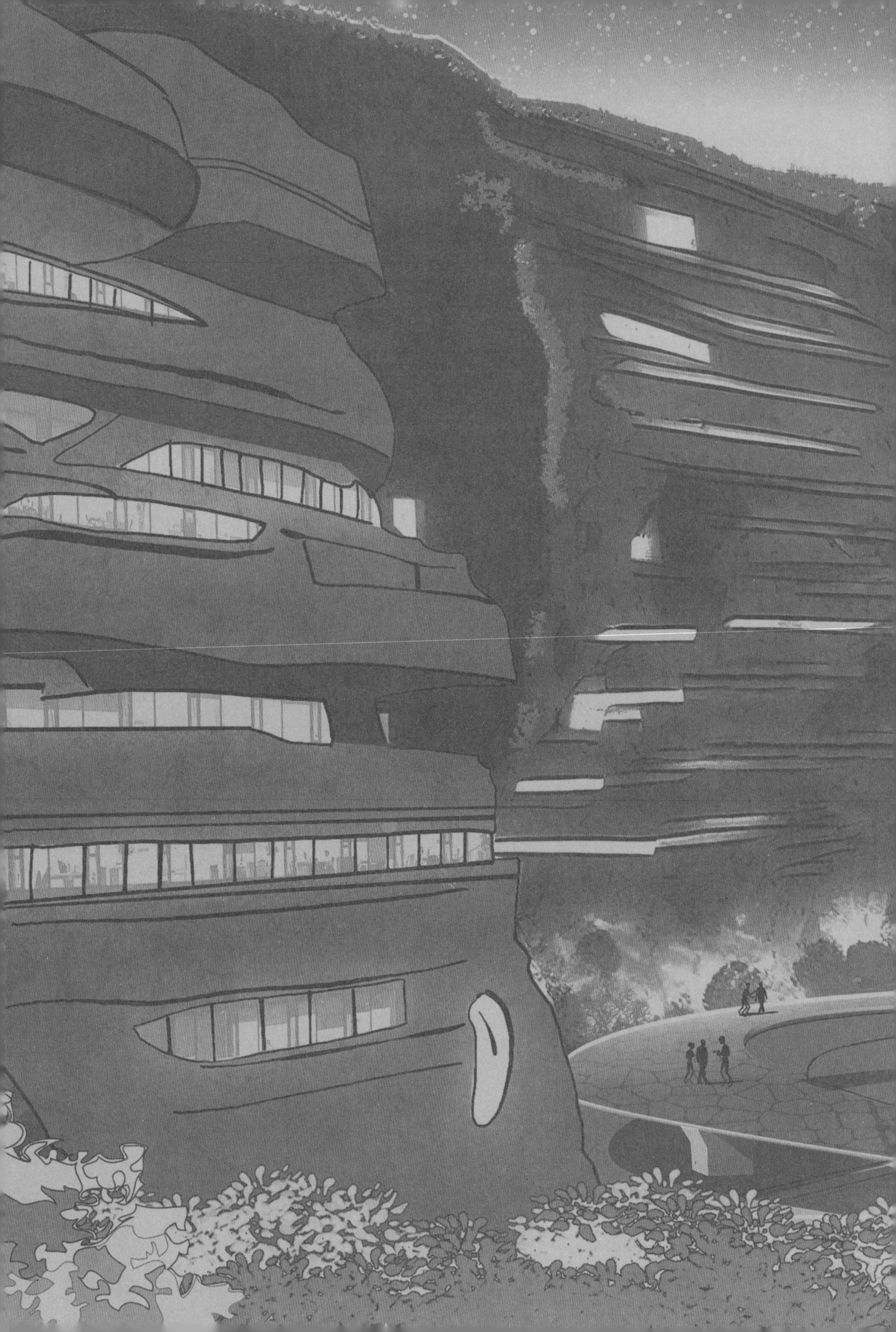